# *An Affair with* HOLLYWOOD

## ROGER NIEZ
### BEN MONA

**ARPress**
45 Dan Road Suite 5
Canton MA 02021

Hotline:      1(888) 821-0229
Fax:          1(508) 545-7580

Ordering Information:

Quantity sales. Special discounts are available on quantity purchases by corporations, associations, and others. For details, contact the publisher at the address above.

Printed in the United States of America.

ISBN-13:
Softcover     979-8-89330-220-2
eBook         979-8-89330-219-6

Library of Congress Control Number: 2024900537

*"While the whole world is mad, I want to watch through
rose-colored glasses…"*


—The Doctor

# CONTENTS

# PROLOGUE

These are true stories of a bodyguard and limo driver working during the height of male chauvinism in the historic 1980s. These stories recall various escapades and sex scandals that have gone unsurfaced for more than forty years, casting light upon the exploitation and subculture in the film industry at the time. As a young bodyguard and limousine driver, these surreal firsthand encounters were simply viewed as executing a job. Despite the context and graphic recollection of these stories, in no way is the behavior or conversations in this book condoned. Out of respect for the dead, some of the names mentioned in this book have been changed or unspecified.

The era during the rise of Blockbuster, MTV, and New Wave music has changed our lives forever. The Cold War had just ended and personal computers were just starting to become available. While Ronald Reagan was president, we witnessed increasing usage of technology and changes in culture. It was an amazing time in history that is remembered for its extreme party lifestyle and participation with sex and drugs.

Roger recalls his assignments and life surrounding Hollywood during the 1980s. His personal relationships with clients, and his interactions with wishful young actresses, presented him with a medium into the party scene… and what was truly going on with this sexually charged era. Throughout these stories, Roger dives headfirst into exploring the Hollywood scene and the mindsets involved during the peak of the casting couch, favor making, and drug usage.

To help further portray each chapter's significance, a song that sets the mood in the eighties and its artist are stated at the beginning of each chapter.

# CHAPTER 1

# THE BODYGUARD

*"Walk This Way" by Run-DMC and Aerosmith*

The sex and drug culture was everywhere in the 1960s, from San Francisco to New York City. The "free love" movement, Vietnam, and rock and roll was the era I was born into. Clashes between hippies and conservatives were in the news all the time. Plays and movies began pushing the moralities of the conservative era ever since the late fifties and early sixties. Even Breakfast at Tiffany's was about a writer having an affair with a married woman, and it involved a young country girl using her looks to make her way into the big city. It is one of my favorite movies, but little did I know how relevant it would become.

By the time the early eighties began, the rich and famous would dress provocatively and everyone had become involved with the new way of partying. There was an aggressive permutation developing among men to have the ultimate sex with the most beautiful women, using their power and influence to get into their pants. Manipulation, name-dropping, and lies became prevalent and normalized within society.

By 1984, I was reintroduced to the Doctor that had delivered me as a baby in 1960. The dear Doctor was a good friend of my family and was my mother's gynecologist from the late fifties to the early sixties, until she moved to Orange County. We were invited to the Doctor's son's wedding in Los Angeles, California. Here I was at a true Hollywood wedding with a very cool crowd of people. The Doctor's girlfriend was approximately twenty years younger than him, and her friends were even younger. As a young twenty-four-year-old, I was impressed with the Doctor and looked up to him as a role model. I had just finished bodyguard school and I was training for high-risk assignments. While I was not former military or law enforcement, domestic bodyguarding for Hollywood's wealthy paid well. With a newly received gun permit and a black belt in karate, I believed I was ready to take up the task of becoming a bodyguard.

The dear Doctor finally mentioned to me that I should come in to his office one day in the future and discuss my career path. Because of his relationship with my parents, and the fact that he delivered me, I was malleable and ripe to be molded by him. He needed a driver and someone he could rely on for various assignments. He preferred to have someone that he could trust and someone that didn't want to make it big in the movies. Only later did I realize that my duties would become the center of the Hollywood scene, intertwined with over-the-top parties and young aspiring actresses.

I showed up to the Doctor's office on a Saturday and his girlfriend was there: a tall, amazing blonde woman. But she was not the usual bimbo girlfriend. She was educated and had an MBA from USC. She traveled the world with the Doctor and ran the real estate side of his large holdings. She was really cool, a beautiful lover and companion. The Doctor offered to pay me to teach her and her best friend self-defense once a week for six months. Aside from the self-defense lessons, I began to drive and do odd jobs for the Doctor. He had taken me under his wing, and in return, I became a loyal and devoted bodyguard for him.

Roger in bodyguard training for the 1984 Winter Olympics.

# CHAPTER 2

# SUNSET PLAZA DRIVE

*"Opposites Attract" by Paula Abdul*

I moved into a luxurious three-story home on Sunset Plaza Drive, owned by the Doctor and his Producer friend. The top level was a master bedroom, where the Doctor or Producer's trophy girlfriend stayed. The middle level was where I lived, commonly used for cooking and entertaining. The lower level had three bedrooms, a large bathroom, and a small den. These three lower level bedrooms were commonly cycled amongst up-and-coming actresses that happened to be dating the Producer's friends or business connections at the time. They were allowed to have people over, but they weren't allowed to have any other men spend the night.

One of the reasons I received free rent at the home was because when I came home late most nights, I was supposed to spy on the lower level and report any infractions. The women that did not make the cut would get a simple offer: they could leave with a plane ticket home, or just leave. About 50 percent of the time they just left on bad terms, while the other 50 percent accepted the ticket home. At no time was this a brothel, and the women were not prostitutes. These were new, handpicked women that came to Hollywood to try and make it big.

Some of the women did not stay long. It was competitive amongst young, up-and-coming actresses in Hollywood. However, they usually traveled in groups just as their sponsors preferred… a good way to have three beautiful women at your convenience at any time (kind of a knockoff of the Playboy Mansion). Not all the women were naive. They knew that this arrangement was a possible way to meet some of the coolest people in Hollywood and they were picked to go to all the mainstream parties. I would drive them by limousine to high-class clubs and events  like Whisky a Go Go, the Rainbow Room, and the Academy Awards if they were fortunate enough to become their sponsor's trophy girlfriend.

Over the years, I had seen a couple of these actresses cast as extras or small roles in blockbuster films. Naturally this gave the Producer, and people of power in Hollywood, authority when talking to these up-and-coming actresses that needed a place to stay. I remember that the Producer always told me he "never paid for the pussy," meaning he compensated them with favors instead of cash. In his mind, a gentleman took care of his girlfriends by introducing them to other sleazy guys. Ultimately, these corrupt men of power could advance these young women's careers if they were slept with in return. Unfortunately, many of these women awoke in the morning after a drug-induced night of debauchery, sometimes willing and sometimes not. Only a small percentage of these actresses were able to further their careers in return.

# CHAPTER 3

# SEX, DRUGS, AND ROCK AND ROLL

*"Welcome to the Jungle" by Guns N' Roses*

As a baby boomer born in 1960, my generation knows sex, drugs, and rock and roll as just a metaphor to living a fun and productive life. But it is true that many people took it literally and had lots of sex and did lots of drugs! Weed, acid, cocaine, heroin, speed, downers, and of course alcohol… all kinds of drugs. After all, these were the same young soldiers in Vietnam that were experimenting with opiates. It became common to mix drugs and other substances with overindulgence in sex. Rock and roll was just the music of the time, growing more and more popular as a movement with many styles. During the transition from folk music to hard rock, everyone was feeling free and excited. Many increased their drug usage and mixed it in with their short- or long-term sexual relationships. It wasn't long until this saying became a massive movement.

Harsher laws began to develop as the movement progressed. Drugs were highly illegal in those days, much more than now. One joint could land you in jail, and the conservative establishment did not find the movement interesting or amusing. These hardworking baby boomers were focused on home and family values, and they were often highly religious. However, here are the facts: College students away from their families for the first time are looking to explore their lives. They all wanted to enjoy sex and drugs while listening to rock and roll. Hippies began to research and emulate the drug and sex history of

Asian and other non-Western countries. The beatniks grew up in coffee shops, calling themselves intellectuals. Oftentimes, they would hang out around college and beach areas with time on their hands to learn poetry, anthropology, and philosophy.

The working class enjoyed the buzz of being able to work hard and play harder. I learned a saying from the Doctor: "I could resist anything but temptation." Oh boy, was there lots of temptation! With birth control on the rise, women could explore sex without the fear of getting pregnant. Women were an equal to men when it came to exploring the new growing movement that was sweeping the nation.

Sex addiction became prevalent in the eighties and has only increased since then. Similarly, mainstream music has evolved to new heights and so has drug usage. Rock and roll shifted more toward hip-hop and techno, while amphetamines, LSD, and heroin have become increasingly more popular. All these components can be used to fuel temptations in young people or people with compulsive addictive personalities. Today we still have college students, politicians, priests, and celebrities being tried in court for rape and sexual assault. Hollywood was just one platform for sexually driven people to carry out their compulsions… and not always in a productive or loving way. It hurt many people and made life more difficult for those who were unfortunate enough to be abused by it.

# CHAPTER 4

# HOLLYWOODLAND

*"Magic" by The Cars*

In 1923, when films were still being made in black and white, the original "Hollywood" sign was actually "Hollywoodland" because land developers were promoting the city for real estate purposes. Later in 1949, when housing development was no longer a priority, the "land" portion of the sign was removed. Although the sign had physically changed, the symbolism of the sign remained intact and is still prominent even today. The origin of the term, "Hollywood," derives literally from the wood of a holly tree; a tree historically known in mythology and witchcraft for having magical capabilities. Hollywood has always been a place intended to aspire people to make their dreams come true. It promoted the impression that this was an exceptional city where magic became reality. Even the buildings in Hollywood and Beverly Hills were built to reflect this notion. This conception was rampant in the eighties, and coincidentally I was able to witness it firsthand during my time in Los Angeles.

Throughout the world, Hollywood had become known as a destination spot for people to fulfill their life journey. Some of the most famous landmarks and attractions that people would want to go to included the Playboy Club, the Hollywood Wax Museum, the Capital Records Building, and Grauman's Chinese Theatre (also known as the TCL Chinese Theatre). Whenever driving for clients or people coming from out of town, I would remind them to walk down

Sunset Boulevard or Hollywood Boulevard so that they could check out the various souvenir shops or the Hollywood Walk of Fame. In the hills, the Griffith Observatory and the Hollywood Sign attracted large crowds of people during all hours.

A large part of the "magical" essence in Hollywood and Beverly Hills was drawn from the hotels alone. Dating back to the 1920s, Los Angeles hotels had become known for the actors and presidents that stayed at them. Many people stayed at or visited these hotels just in hopes of maybe getting a glimpse of a famous star or elite that happened to be staying there. The Roosevelt Hotel, Beverly Hills Hotel, Beverly Wilshire Hotel, and the Ambassador Hotel were just a few hotels that were known to attract famous actors, producers, politicians, and international celebrities. Each hotel had its own intriguing architecture, personality, history, and vibe that left an everlasting impression upon you.

There was no shortage of people or things to do in Hollywood and Los Angeles, but it was never considered a "real" trip to Hollywood unless you cruised the Sunset Strip at night. Gangsters, glamour girls, and other notorious types of people have walked the Sunset Strip for over half a century while fueling Hollywood's whimsical reputation. Clubs, restaurants, and events were always packed, and the people that came out at night were shameless and bizarre. The nightlife mixed with all the neon and bright lights made walking the streets at night seem like a surreal illusion. From older venues like the Hollywood Bowl or the Hollywood Palladium to newer attractions like Universal Studios, business was always booming. Tour companies were even offering attractions and private tours to view famous stars and their homes. It was as if all these individual attractions were put together to create one big show in itself… a show that seemingly never ended.

# CHAPTER 5

# THE FAVOR

*'Thriller" by Michael Jackson*

In business and politics, you say, "You scratch my back and I will scratch yours," meaning if you help me in advance, I will help you in the future. But it was Hollywood in the eighties that really made this saying a mastery of manipulation and a control of power. One example was a casting director that would help someone get into a movie role from the referral of a friend that they knew.

Yes, favoritism was rampant in Hollywood. The typical favor of actors, producers, and directors using their friends or family in films is of course normal. But let me take you down the road that everyone doesn't want to talk about... The big elephant in the room. Many times, a young actor or actress would be put in a position where they became of sexual interest to those in power. A movie would have a casting call, so the talent would get a private interview with a casting director or producer. No matter their talent or star quality, it was not uncommon for the casting call to lead to a direct hookup.

The talent would often have the choice to have sex with the person of power in exchange for a role in a movie. Was this exploitation or just good business for both sides? There were several times when I was sent to pick up a young, beautiful actress that had only been in Hollywood for a short time. They would take acting classes and practice its craft, but at the end, someone she met always wanted a favor in return for helping them. Most of the time the talent would assume what that favor would be, but there were times when it was their first encounter with the dirty secret in Hollywood.

How bad do you want to make it in the film industry? You may dance well or be a truly talented actress, but unless you gave someone a blowjob or sexual favor, you may be waiting all day for a casting call that only allows you three minutes to try and land a role. Then you would be notified that someone else landed the part. Yes, someone else just cashed in on a sexual favor that you either refused or bypassed!

One day, I was paged to pick up a young woman, so I drove to the Sunset Plaza home and picked her up. She had her portfolio and headshots with her, and she was dressed in a classic 1980s leather and lace outfit. She got in the back of the limo and I let her know that anything in the minibar was hers to use. She was so cheerful and excited to be taken to the Producer's home to be interviewed for a small role in a B-movie. We pulled up to the Producer's house and she walked up to his door. In she went and I was instructed to wait as long as the interview took.

After forty minutes, the front door opened and the woman came out. Her head was down and she walked fast toward my limo. I opened the limo door for her and we started heading back to the Sunset Plaza home. Even with the interior window rolled up, I could hear her crying in the back seat. Suddenly, the window rolled down and she asked if I could drive a little faster. I told her that I drive the speed limit, but I will do the best that I can for her. She was now a mess… shaking with tears running down her face. I did not want to start a conversation, but I was so intrigued. I asked, "Would you like to discuss the casting call?" She replied, "I never want to go back to that place ever again. That man was a pig. P.I.G. I will most likely not get the part from that fucking asshole." She asked me if I drove to the Producer's house often and I told her that this was the third time this month.

After returning to the Sunset Plaza home, I asked the actress if she would be okay. She said, "Yes. I understand now that I have been a naïve girl. This town is not what I thought it would be at all." I listened to her talk about coming to Hollywood from Canada and hoping to land a part as an actress. I tried to explain to her that I did not know much about the industry, but it seemed like it required hard work, connections, and years of practice. She smiled and said, "Yes, and fucking your way in."

It was 11 a.m. the next morning when I was paged to go back and pick up the same young lady. I pulled up to the Sunset Plaza house and her bags were already packed outside. She got in the car and I was told to take her to LAX airport. The Doctor had gotten a call from the Producer, and as a favor to the Producer, they gave the actress the classic ultimatum: move out with a plane ticket back home, or just move out. She chose the plane ticket home.

Favors were everywhere and it became a currency that flowed throughout Hollywood. Aside from being widely used to obtain sex and drugs, all types of services and products were traded and used to gain an advantage. If it was not about being in a movie, soap, or sitcom, favors were used by the rich to help further their career or get deals done. I saw very little money actually pass hands in the film industry. A favor would be used and a drug prescription would be written, or a young and beautiful woman would show up at your house. Maybe a favor would be used to get a new suit or a new microwave from the warehouse. It was like a Goodfellas mob commerce of goods and products being traded for favors.

# CHAPTER 6

# NICHOLS CANYON

*"Tainted Love" by Soft Cell*

Nichols Canyon Road is one of the most infamous streets in Hollywood, known as a large hill containing the homes of many well-known movie stars and wealthy people. It could have a doctor, superstar, upstanding citizen, and even a porn star all on the same street. The Nichols Canyon lore is amazing! During Prohibition, there was a cylinder building at the end of the street that was a meeting place for gambling, socializing, and of course partying. When the lights from the police coming up the hill could be seen, it gave everyone time to scatter and destroy or hide the booze. Although many years have passed since then, the same affluent lifestyle has been upheld there.

One morning in 1985, I was prepared to pick up the Doctor from his Nichols Canyon home. Driving back down the hill, we realized that the police had raided a home many houses down. The police had helicopters flying around and several cars blocking the street, certainly not letting anyone by. As we waited over an hour to pass and get down the hill, the Doctor and I figured that there had to have been a murder. That day, the news reported that a famous actor was visiting his brother's home on Nichols Canyon and that the police had raided it for cocaine. Apparently, after a wild night of partying with several young ladies, some neighbors decided to call the police and report a noise complaint. When the cops arrived, it wasn't long until the noise complaint escalated into a cocaine bust. I'll never forget that it was on a typical Wednesday night.

A blonde woman awakes in the middle of the night, lying naked near a fireplace with her legs spread open. She sees a black smoking jacket lying on a chair beside her, similar to the Playboy Mansion jacket worn by Hugh Hefner. She reaches into one of the jacket pockets, finds a loaded .38 snub-nosed revolver, and cocks the hammer back. As a shadowed figure comes out of the doorway from the bathroom toward the fireplace, it notices the naked blonde with the gun and immediately dives behind a nearby loveseat to avoid her aim. The naked woman fires the gun at him as she screams, "You fucked me in my ass!" The man jumps up from behind cover, runs to the woman, and grabs the gun from out of her hand. The woman passes out.

My pager went off at 4:00 a.m. with "911" after the return number, meaning it was an emergency. I jumped in the limo and drove to Nichols Canyon Road. I arrived at the Doctor's house and there was Missy, a woman I had met at several parties and driven to the Producer's house before, opening the door for me. Missy was naked, wasted, and smelling of alcohol. "Good morning, Missy." She looked at me with a glazed look as if she had been up all night on drugs. I went inside the home and she started getting dressed right in front of me. First her panties, then her sundress, before picking up her high-heeled pumps and carrying them out with her overnight bag. I helped her into the limo and as we started to head out, I saw a small .38 caliber hole in the sliding glass window of the living room. I went back into the house and the Doctor was on the phone, trying to get a glass company to come fix the window. He explained the incident to me and told me to return after I dropped Missy off. Back down Nichols Canyon I drove, wondering how many other bizarre events were going on in the other houses on this street.

Shortly afterward, I moved into the orange room of the Nichols Canyon home as the Doctor's bodyguard and personal assistant. Each room had its own color and theme. For example, the red room was the master bedroom and the blue room was the guest bedroom with blue fish statues. The house had a Machiavellian feel to it with bookshelves consisting of medical, spiritual, martial arts, neurolinguistic programming, and hypnosis books. In any case, the house was amazing with its seven-foot-tall reproductions of the Easter Island heads overlooking the black-bottomed pool. The property contained a tennis court and even had a trophy room, full of taxidermied animals from the Doctor's hunting safaris in Africa. As unfortunate as Missy's conundrum was, I was thankful that she had unintentionally provided me with such an opulent home to live in.

# CHAPTER 7

# THE CASTING COUCH

*"Another One Bites the Dust" by Queen*

Following the Doctor's orders, one day I drove a rental truck down Western Avenue to an oriental furniture store. When I showed up, the storage office manager asked me for my ID. When I gave it to him, he smiled and told me to drive to the back. The Doctor had given him my name and told him that I would be the one picking up his furniture. We loaded the truck with expensive Chinese dynasty-red furniture, such as chairs, a love seat, a carved dressing screen, and carved coffee tables. However, the most memorable piece of dynasty-red furniture that we loaded was a large leather couch. I drove the furniture to a film studio lot, where the Doctor had rented a small office.

I opened the door to the office and realized that the space was not that fancy, but it was freshly painted. I began moving the heavy dynasty-red furniture into the office. I was dripping in sweat by the time the Doctor drove up with the Producer. Two beautiful women got out of their car, dressed in leather pants and lacy tops… totally eighties. They had red lips, perfect makeup, large breasts, and thin waists. One of the women was introduced as the Producer's interior designer, but she was nothing like the educated interior designers I had met at parties. In short, based upon our conversation, I got the impression that this woman was not really sophisticated. But they went to work, moving the furniture around and taking pictures. After a couple of hours, we had a good-looking meeting place with the large leather couch at the center of attention.

I said my goodbyes and took the truck back to the rental yard. Afterward, I went back to our office on Western Avenue and waited downstairs for the Doctor. About three hours later, the Doctor showed up and told me that I would get a bonus on my next paycheck. As we started walking upstairs to the office, he turned to me and said, "Those girls were the best fuck ever!" I said the only thing I could say, "I'm glad you like the new office." The office became known as the "Casting Couch Office," and it was just that if anything.

The Doctor loved that little studio lot office. He only had it for a short time, but he would always deploy me to pick people up in the limo and bring them by. Both he and the Producer used the office to bring friends, or people to impress, over to meet and discuss scripts. However, the office's main usage was intended for casting calls and seducing actresses. On many occasions, I would pick up young actresses and bring them to the office. It was amazing how excited the women would get when we drove through the arches of the front gate with "Studio Lot" engraved on them.

The office stocked a full bar and, while no drugs were allowed on the location, the visitors always seemed to be packing. Cocaine was the drug of choice and was common with some cocktails on the side. Many of the women I picked up from the office asked to be dropped off at their favorite club or restaurant, where they had other friends awaiting them. Most of the time the women had a good buzz going and wanted to keep the party alive. Also, it definitely went with the scene to have a limo pull up to you after attending a casting call… It made the women think that they actually obtained a part in a film, as opposed to the reality of being chauffeured away after a one-night stand.

I have to say, it was head-spinning to keep track of who was using the office when both the Doctor and the Producer would loan it to their friends. I counted more than seven keys replicated for the office and casually cycled around. The Doctor even asked me to do some surveillance over a two-day period, just to make sure that people were not taking advantage of the office. He was worried that the studio lot owners would cancel the lease at any moment because demand was high to get the smallest offices on the lot. With no surprise, on the first day I counted four different people using the office to have several appointments with young women. They would go into the office with a woman for 45 minute intervals and then leave. It was not long after until we closed the office, but the Doctor made sure to move the dynasty-red furniture to the Sunset Plaza home.

# CHAPTER 8

# THE LIMO

> "Drive" by The Cars

The limousine has always been known as a status symbol for wealth and prestige. Those that were famous always had more than one person in the limo with them, whether it was a driver, a couple bodyguards, or an entourage of people. However, the most admired aspect about limos was the ability to have privacy in the passenger area. You could party, watch TV, have a personal discussion, and even have sex in a limo without anyone batting an eye. It goes without saying that the limo was not only a device for transportation, but also a powerful right that often reflected your social status.

The limo was a party wagon and a place where people could entertain themselves and others. The things that you could do in the back seat… We all know people had sex in limos, but when the bad girls knew they had to put out for an amazing time out in the town, they would get right to it. After the shows, parties, or events, the drugs kicked in and the orgies started. I was so surprised the first time one of my clients and a few women he was with did not roll up the tinted privacy window separating the driver from the back area. Knowing I could elevate the window from the driver's side, I asked them, "Would you like the window up?" They just looked deadpan at me and replied, "Why?" So if you think texting and driving is dangerous, you have not driven a limo as a twenty-five-year-old man with three gorgeous and naked women having an orgy in the back seat.

So let me go on the record right now. I never fucked any of those gals, even though several times they wanted me to. However, many times I did use the limo off-duty for my private use. Can you imagine me picking up my girlfriend from college in a limo to go out for a date? I was so lucky to have a Cadillac and Lincoln limousine at twenty-five and twenty-six years old.

One night, I was driving for a really creepy client. He was a friend of the Producer's and had asked him as a favor to borrow the limo. His favor was granted with one exception: he had to tip me when the night was completed. I arrived at a hotel in downtown Los Angeles around 7:00 p.m., and he was waiting in the lobby. I was holding my black chalkboard, which I used to greet passengers I had not known, with "Mr. Finkle" written on it. An overweight Jewish guy in his sixties approached me. He had curly gray hair, wore a light-colored suit with an expensive blue sweatshirt, and had shoes with no socks. This guy was so high on coke that he couldn't hide it.

I opened the passenger door and Mr. Finkle rolled into the back seat. He was a good-natured guy who spoke well and always had a smile on his face. He poured himself a scotch on the rocks before pulling a small envelope out of his pocket. With no straw, he put his nose in the envelope and inhaled a huge amount of cocaine. He wiped the white residue off the top of his nose with his hand before licking it, just like a scene out of Scarface. Fuck, this guy had a snort nearly every fifteen minutes. I was scared that we might get busted, but mainly scared because I thought he was going to overdose in the back seat of my limo.

We drove up to an enormous house off Mulholland, which had an extravagant front door. I walked up to the house and rang the doorbell. About five minutes went by, which felt like thirty minutes standing in front of this colossal mansion. Suddenly, a number of high-pitched voices talking and laughing came closer from inside. The door opened up and there they were: two blondes and a black woman dressed as hookers. However, despite their looks, something told me that they were not call girls but some new women set up for Mr. Finkle by the Producer. They went straight to the limo and started drinking everything in the minibar fridge and the ice bucket. I was instructed to cruise Sunset Boulevard. When the privacy window rolled down to give me continued driving instructions, all three women had their tops off and were already wasted. It was nothing that I hadn't seen before, except there was a weird disconnect with me. Mr. Finkle, gray-haired and not very attractive, had his pants half off and was getting a blowjob from one of the blondes. The black gal seemed disinterested in Mr. Finkle and kept wanting to talk to me through the lowered privacy window.

As we turned onto Western Avenue, the women asked me to go back to Sunset Boulevard. They wanted to go to Coconut Teasers, a known nightclub with high-energy bands and dancing… It was way too young of a place for Mr. Finkle, but I turned the limo around and drove them to the location. They all jumped out of the limo and went into the club except the second blonde, who decided not to go. I parked the limo and walked down the street to get a cup of coffee. When I returned to the club, the second blonde was standing outside of the back door while smoking a cigarette. I asked her if she needed anything and she said, "Yes. To get out of here. Like fucking now." I asked her if she would like to be dropped off somewhere, but she said, "No. I stick with my friends even though they are being stupid tonight. That guy tried to put his finger in my ass…" She was taking a drag from her cigarette when I asked her what was going on. She explained that her friends wanted to party tonight, and she confirmed my suspicion that the Producer set them up with his accountant, Mr. Finkle. Forty-five minutes later, Mr. Finkle and the two women came out of the nightclub and piled back into the limo. The ride back to the hotel consisted of Mr. Finkle doing coke, unable to keep his hands off the black woman.

When I dropped them off at the hotel, Mr. Finkle slipped me $100 while stumbling away with the black woman and the first blonde. The second blonde was still in the back of the limo, and she asked, "Can you take me home now?" I told her that it was my job to, and she rode in the front seat while I drove her home. She told me about moving from Canada with her friend and where they met the other black woman. "She loves a good time, but that guy was a pig." I was trying to have a serious conversation with her, but I finally broke out laughing and said,

"I hate to be cliché, but what is a beautiful girl like you doing in a place like this?" She finally gave me a smile and said, "I'm just lucky, I guess."

There were many odd nights when I was instructed to use the limo to pick up strangers who had never met each other before. Oftentimes, the ratio of older men to younger women was one to three. At least one of the women was usually loaded, drugged, or easy enough for the older man to have a one-night stand with. The limo was just a tool to get laid… like a hammer for a framer, a pen for an attorney, or a lab coat for a doctor.

# CHAPTER 9

# THE DEAR DOCTOR

*"I Wanna Dance with Somebody ( Who Loves Me )"*
*by Whitney Houston*

The Doctor was born in 1925 and was the son of a Greek hotel operator. He started out washing dishes and married young while working in the family business. He was accustomed to hard work and a controlling father, who was abusive and had an iron-fisted personality. At an older age, he realized that he could make substantial amounts of money and influence as a doctor of medicine. As his ambitions grew, it became apparent that the only way he would get ahead in life was to become a doctor. However, after the Doctor graduated with his degree, the success and strain on his marriage produced a divorce. He hardly drank and never did drugs, though he did have an addiction to gorgeous women. He had sex with beautiful women of all types, from little people to one-legged females, just to not leave anything untouched. His biggest weakness was tall blondes, but he was not selective if they were twenty-three or younger.

Ironically, the Doctor became a gynecologist.... so he saw nearly ten to twenty vaginas every week. He purchased an office building on Western Avenue and custom-built it to have a perfect floor plan of five thousand square feet. He built over twenty exam rooms, a private office, a bathroom, and of course a safe closet to keep his valuables. His waiting room was large and was often full to the maximum capacity. He was actually an excellent doctor when it came to diagnosis. He had a certain talent to know what was wrong with a patient long before their lab results came back.

The Doctor lived his life large and had the money to do so, traveling to all the exotic places on the planet. He could function on five hours of sleep and even when I was forty years younger than him, I still could not keep up. He often wore a black velvet coat and silky black slacks, all well-fitting. Regarding jewelry, he was way ahead of Mr. T in flash and bling. He wore a large gold chain and extravagant rings, one of which looked like a Super Bowl ring in size but was perfectly shaped as a lion's head. Aside from the Cadillac limousine that the Doctor had me drive, he loved sports cars, owned a collection of them, and used them to their maximum capacity. He had three Mustangs, a Vintage T-bird, a two-door Mercedes, and a Cadillac Fleetwood. The dear Doctor loved nightclubs and dancing. Whenever he was at a club, he would never sit for long. In his sixties, he paid the top break-dancer in Los Angeles to teach him how to break-dance… At the time, the Doctor and I were excited to be the only two white guys break-dancing in high-end clubs. To start off his night, he would usually eat light and only have one top-shelf drink. His night would always end with him getting laid; even as a 65-year-old, he was a dying romantic. He never missed birthdays or special occasions to party, and he could coordinate multiple events all while running a large medical practice. In many ways he was an extremely amazing human, working ten to fifteen hours a day while sustaining an outgoing nightlife.

About a year before Quaaludes were taken off the market, the Doctor had foresight and purchased around five thousand tabs of them. He leased three separate storage lockers, each about one mile from his office. He filled two of these lockers with personal items from his life, such as furniture, paintings, clothes, and of course the Quaaludes divided up along with thousands of pictures of naked women. These images weren't professional pornographic pictures, but simply Polaroid shots of women with open legs or breasts showing. Somehow the Doctor knew I was a honest guy, and being loyal as hell to him, he knew I would never care to steal from or show anyone the storage units.

The Doctor was my main client and he loved the fast, intense, sexually charged lifestyle in Hollywood. He did not do anything without a plan;

but when he did wing it, he pushed the limits of the moment. One night, he had crashed his sports car while trying to drive home after having plastic surgery. He blew out a tire and drove all the way back home on the rim, sparks flying everywhere. On a separate occasion, he was pulled over and the police found his small .38 caliber revolver that he always carried. He was arrested, but immediately released after a judge friend helped reduce the charge. Apparently, the judge had owed him a favor for all the years that the Doctor had introduced him to young women and allowed him to use his homes and cars. There was never a dull moment when working or hanging out around the dear Doctor.

# CHAPTER 10

# DOUBLE-EDGED SWORD

*"Jump" by Van Halen*

I was instructed to meet with a new client, one of the Doctor's old friends. Ms. Williams was a successful Hollywood realtor and about forty-three years old. She was redheaded and very well-dressed at all times. I met her at a restaurant near Universal Studios. We had a nice lunch, and she explained to me that she would like to have a bodyguard to keep her protected at night and during some house tours when she was waiting for clients to arrive. There had been several robberies in the prior month when realtors in large mansions had cash, a Rolex, and gold jewelry taken from them... the robbers knowing the large homes attracted wealthy people. She lived alone and offered to provide me room and board in her back house in exchange for me being an armed bodyguard on her property. Sunset Plaza was finally changing to a rental home, so I figured this was a suitable agreement.

On the first week, it was like a good roommate relationship. She paid me by the hour while also providing me free rent for staying at her home. When I entered her house one night, she had a bottle of wine open and was on her second glass. She asked me how my day was, and I noticed that she had no bra on and that her low-cut dress was almost falling off her shoulders. We had a couple of beers in the main house before we moved to the couch, where we continued to talk. I noticed she had her legs a little open and that she was wearing attractive panties that I could easily see. I looked right at her open top and spread legs like the naive 25-year-old I was. She saw I was looking and said, "Let's have a kiss?" I remember getting closer and closer to her until we were embraced in a kiss. Too weak to turn her down, before I knew it, I picked her up and took her to the bedroom. Now that I look back on it, this had to have been some sort of fantasy for her… A woman in her early forties having sex with a guy in his twenties.

The next morning, I told Ms. Williams that I hoped last night didn't change anything but I would understand if she wanted me to move out. She said it was fine and that she would like for us to remain as friends with benefits. This went on for about two weeks until one morning, I got up early for work for an important meeting with a new client. I had just jumped into my car when I noticed that she was on the porch, staring at me. I popped my head out of the car window and told her I was off to the office. She called back out to me, asking why I had snuck out and not made love to her. Taken aback by the question, I told her that I just had to get going. She responded, saying that when I came back that night to please pack up my bags and move out. I was fine with this because I felt she was just using me as a boy toy with a .45 Colt to protect her. She was always good to me, but she was way too authoritative and wanted to call all the shots.

See, women of power in Hollywood had the same drives and egos that the men of power did. While mostly men contained power in the eighties, the women in power felt even more determined to abuse their power as a way of asserting their dominance. Although Ms. Williams was successful and had much influence, she was a control freak and it was just a matter of time until our relationship ended… Just like the cycling relationship my clients had with the young actresses they dated. Two weeks after moving out, I had lunch with Ms. Williams again. She was determined to convince me to move back in with her and try out our agreement again. I declined her offer, but she took it well. We were still friends whenever we ran into each other around town or mutual clients.

I was doing odd jobs and driving for a famous casting director that worked for a popular daytime soap opera in the 1980s. Marvin was a short Jewish guy in his sixties, and he was always very nice to me. The Doctor asked him as a favor to see if I could get an atmosphere part on his soap opera. So instead of paying me directly, one week after each of my assignments, Marvin would call me up to offer me an atmosphere part on the soap opera. I ended up doing several atmosphere parts for the soap, and the pay rate was approximately $259 for half the day's pay. Back then, that was good money for side work and a chance to be on television.

One afternoon, Marvin asked me to come to his home to move boxes. He had wall-to-wall boxes with movie and television scripts, along with Hollywood pictures and posters in every room. Everything was really cluttered, but the boxes were organized by year and type of production. It got to be around 5:00 p.m., and I had to go pick the women up from Sunset Plaza Drive for a big party. I asked Marvin if I could get showered and dressed at his home, and he said that would be fine. I showered and when I went to get out of the shower, I saw no towels in the bathroom. So I yelled out to Marvin, "Any towels?" Marvin appeared in the doorway with a single washcloth, only a few inches wide. I awkwardly dried myself with the washcloth while he watched. After that incident, I didn't receive anymore soap opera roles or driving assignments from Marvin. I mentioned the event to the Doctor, and he jokingly said I would have gotten a speaking part if I blew the guy. Although it was a joke, I am sure he was right. I knew how those things could happen in that circle of favors.

Men had the same sexual harassment and awkward situations in Hollywood as women during the eighties. However, women received more of it and were more likely to get "wined, dined, and sixty-nined," as the old saying goes. Of course, this was the era that was popular for the word gigolo, a guy who gets paid for having sex with rich women. But how many times do you think the guys were paid to be sex slaves or treated as a pet? You know how women love their pets—as long as they're obedient and well behaved.

Roger's headshots for acting gigs.

# CHAPTER 11

# CAN YOU SPELL QUAALUDE?

---

*"White Rabbit" by Jefferson Airplane*

---

The prevalence of drugs in the 1980s revamped the war on drugs and the "Just Say No" campaign movement. Other than pot and cocaine, pharmaceutical drugs were well-known in Hollywood. Everything from uppers to downers had hooked so many people from the entertainment industry. Many celebrities have overdosed by mixing so many different drugs that they get heart attacks, seizures, and then just don't wake up... We often hear about similar incidents in the modern day.

The drug that dominated its time in the late seventies and early eighties was Quaaludes, which were taken off the market in 1984. In 1951, Quaaludes were originally created to treat malaria. But they weren't officially patented until 1962, when they became prescribed as a sedative to treat anti-depression. However, the user usually ended up having major comedowns and the short break it gave from depression was not warranted. Similar to Valium, Quaaludes provided a hypnotic and euphoric drowsiness upon the user. After many years of research, Quaaludes became decisively renown as a sleeping aid to treat insomnia. It wasn't long until the drug was quickly popularized and abused for its aphrodisiac capabilities.

After its removal from the market, Quaaludes evolved from being pharmaceutically prescribed to being illegally bootlegged... the same way ecstasy found its way to the streets two to three years later.

One of the most common types of parties in Hollywood back then consisted of mixing champagne and Quaaludes. Many people that had never originally taken the drug were quick to think of it as cocaine, presuming it would be fun to take and that it would give out a really good trip. Therefore, Quaaludes were casually used in drinks and foods in abundant amounts. Those naive souls rapidly realized how much they underestimated the intense out-of-body and euphoric experience.

The primary way Quaaludes entered the "elite" film scene in Hollywood was through its usage to gain an unfair advantage of the person it was given to. Quaaludes became regularly used as a date-rape drug; however, they influenced people in different ways than roofies. Instead of making someone pass out right away, Quaaludes made people more likely to consent to sex because of its effects. Quaaludes were therefore commonly deemed as the "perfect fuck drug."

Mixing cocaine and Quaaludes created an uncontrollable party scene, which set the stage for rockers trashing hotel rooms and two day binges never-before-seen. I was with the Sunset Plaza women at a party that lasted four days, with only two or three hours of sleep… They slept with their dates and each other, if you get my drift, but very little actual sleep took place. Sex and then party, party then some more sex. On a different weekend my girlfriend came in from college, and in a seventy-two-hour period we slept for maybe eight hours. The problem was after the effects of the drugs, which induced a big comedown that started with depression and sleep deprivation, and ended with large mood swings.

Hollywood was based off of drama… not just in movies, but the actual lives of these high-strung people just trying to unwind through the use of drugs. One minute women would be happy and stripping down to nothing, then an hour later reality hits them and they want out. Not everyone could handle their drugs and not everyone had overdoses, but many had meltdowns. Guys under the influence would either want to fuck or fight. The arguments between them regarding just about anything could be so strange to watch as a bystander. If you just looked at someone the wrong way, you could unknowingly become a target to fight.

What was happening a lot was that the parties were so over-the top, that most people wanted the fun to never end. So after the party, you would go out to a bar and then usually go hook up with your lover. When the bad guys gave women a Quaalude, the snowballing effect of hours of parties would tire down the women and create an opportunity to take advantage of them. How could the woman say no when they didn't even know if they were living life or having an exotic dream? The next day they would finally realize that it may have been real; and they would feel regretful, pissed off, and naive.

# CHAPTER 12

# FEAR AND LOATHING IN HOLLYWOOD

*"Jessie's Girl" by Rick Springfield*

The yuppies and New Age guys of the eighties were having a lot of fun experiencing the evolving culture. The guys benefited from women now using birth control, makeup, and adventurous attitudes that their mothers would once scorn over. With the reintroduction of miniskirts, low-cut dresses, and slinky bathing suits, many fads objectivized women in the 1980s.

Madonna, the pop star, is currently in her sixties. When I was growing up, women in their sixties did not look like her... even if they were famous. She was the ground zero of the 1980s and the prime example of how sex and controversial lifestyles got the people going. These eccentric but fashionable trends helped pave the way for the punk rock appearance that we all know today. Spiked and dyed hair with leather apparel offered women a new look that reflected their personality, and displayed that they were no longer daddy's little girl. Los Angeles and Hollywood were loved for their acceptance of these changing times and new fashions.

Marilyn Monroe, Mae West, Loretta Swit... Do you see the progression here? There is obviously no excuse for men drugging women and taking advantage of them. However, as Hollywood became intertwined with the sexually charged culture, more and more of these instances recurred. Similar to the homosexual culture that was developing in San Francisco, over time a geographic area develops its reputation or acceptable norms by looking for individual lust and excitement. This is not a reputation that develops overnight, although that is what it felt like in Hollywood during the era of Happy Days or The Waltons, clean and long-running television shows from the seventies and eighties.

By the time MTV came out with music videos containing increased nudity and explicit language, the eighties had accepted them as art and freedom of one's rights. It was evident by this time that art and music had become ripe areas for "sex and drug" lifestyles. Sure, these two things have been affiliated with artists for decades, but drug usage and sexual assault grew drastically in Hollywood during the eighties. Many talented lives were lost or scarred from their lifestyle of extreme living.

Hollywood was used as a venue to live out your fantasies and guilty pleasures during the 1980s. It was considered the opportune place to experience sex, drugs, and alcohol in a party environment. Being the setting of where numerous stories and films were created, Hollywood motivated people to escape from reality and create their own memorable experiences. After all, everyone wanted to escape their dull lives by living out their own personal movies. It was as if people were continuously looking for a new thrill to add to their life each day. Obviously, these numerous attempts to live out whimsical utopias and impractical dreams drove people to do some crazy shit. It became part of the culture to change your look or take on another character. For example, on my father's fiftieth birthday, my mother got him a Dolly Parton look-alike as a singing telegram (because she knew how he loved big-breasted women). This may be viewed as being disrespectful to females, but my mother never took offense to this. My father always treated her as a queen and, in return, my mother treated him as a king. The people in Hollywood were just playing out the roles they had always yearned to experience, no matter how ridiculous or far-fetched they appeared on the surface.

The Hollywood culture was heavily based upon sex appeal in the 1980s, undeniably promoting female sexual objectification. When my clients met a woman they were attracted to, they felt her sexual possibilities were their prize. It was naturally more difficult for women in Hollywood to fit in or obtain a job if they didn't look sexy or attractive. Many men in power abused this changing culture and behaved as if they were entitled to have any woman that they had acquired leverage over… Like children in a candy store, taking what they want without considering the consequences. Mixed with street drugs and the party lifestyle, sexual objectification organically blended with 1980s Hollywood.

# CHAPTER 13

# HEDONISM

*"Push It" by Salt-N-Pepa*

When hedonists were young, they had partners that encouraged them to sleep with others. While these promiscuous relationships may be frowned upon in the modern day, in the 1980s these practices were customarily embraced. Hedonism usually attracted heavily sensual and non-religious people… although many of them would try to tell you that it was their religion. Circulating around the theory that there is no afterlife, hedonists believe that this is the only life you will have as a biological on this planet. Therefore, hedonists believe that you must experience pleasures of the flesh in order to explore as many avenues not pertaining to religious or personal guilt. In short, the primary purpose of hedonism was to have fun by sleeping with many partners and to experience drugs or other stimulants for the mind and body.

While hedonists disregarded karma and whether something was moral or immoral, they did eventually find out that there were negative consequences to their actions. Deriving from the hippies during the "free love" movement in the sixties and seventies, venereal diseases became more and more common among hedonists. Aside from sexually transmitted diseases, pregnancies and the birth of children among these licentious relationships created distress and even more complications upon those following this extreme practice. The newer followers of hedonism gradually began to wrap their head around the fact that there is nothing free in this world… There is a cost to each of your actions.

Oftentimes, the toll upon hedonism wouldn't even be noticed until many years later. In wife-swapping, married couples have sex with other married couples. These couples have love and respect for their partners, but solely seek new and exciting sexual experiences. However, if word got out about these affairs, it was only a matter of time until others began to suffer from these seemingly innocent escapades. Parents that were conservative or monogamous would get upset over it, children that found out would get confused, and your spouse might even fall in love with someone else's partner. Karma had a tendency to come back many years later, simply because you experimented with a sexual thrill one night. Just a hedonistic act alone had the propensity to always be a burden upon your psyche.

Obviously not all people were big drug users, but in the eighties the craziest drugs were culturally everywhere in Los Angeles. It became common among hedonists to mix drugs as a way of enhancing feelings and sexual pleasures. Drugs had the ability to create such extreme simulation, that people would remember the feeling or even have HPPD many years after taking them. Sometimes it would even be these drugs that made the user realize that hedonism does not actually work. Needless to say, hedonism's popularity began to drift away from the culture.

An observation I made among hedonists was that moderation or sobriety would become difficult to achieve, and the ability to function with normal society would seem unattainable. Many times, hedonists going through the eighties influence would come to regret their decisions. They would think that if they had not experienced the culture, maybe they would have settled down with a family earlier or had one less divorce. I know I thought about it after the end of my third long-term relationship.

# CHAPTER 14

# THE MANSIONS

> *"Ghostbusters" by Ray Parker Jr.*

If the paintings in a Hollywood mansion could talk, they still wouldn't be able to find the words to describe the bizarre stories they've witnessed. The Hollywood environment was full of wealth and extravagance, and with it came arrogance and reverie. Anyone that thought nothing was going on behind the walls of a ten-bedroom mansion was ingenuously mistaken. With the homes already full of countless history, the compulsive owners brought out the true eccentricity within Hollywood and Beverly Hills neighborhoods. The conceited mentalities and lifestyles of extreme debauchery set the perfect stage for attracting shady misbehavior.

During the 1980s, the porn industry was transitioning from bushy pubic hair and natural breasts to shaved models and silicone tits. Producers and directors were making so much money, that they naturally began to think that their fantasies could become realities. One of the most common fantasies consisted of owning a big house and having lots of sex in it. Many figured that if they could create a film that people desired, then why couldn't they make that desire an actuality? There have been a lot of ill-minded people in Hollywood that lived their life like this. Men and women alike fed this wave of sex, drugs, and power.

One of the Producer's favorite pastimes was to meet clients at his house with naked and beautiful women lounging around his estate. He would often host guests or take telephone calls while walking around like a playboy in his bathrobe. One day, I was paged to escort a young lady to a party in Beverly Hills. She was a friend of the Producer and had been at his home with three of her girlfriends all day, lying naked around the pool and skinny-dipping. The Producer answered the door and as the young woman was getting her bag ready, the Producer told me, "You have to come out to the pool right now." I followed him outside to the pool and, to my surprise, I found a naked blonde sunbathing facedown on a blanket with her legs wide open. He was so proud and excited to show off his beautiful models, as if they were intended to boost his prestige or my respect for him. He said, "See that! See that! That is my cum dripping out of her pussy!" It was such an awkward and weird situation, but I felt I had to be polite and say something. I responded to him as if he were an infant learning to ride a bike: "Good job…" When the young lady had finished getting her bag, we drove off in the limo. Nothing was spoken about the Producer or his extreme way of living, as if it were just another day in Hollywood.

The young lady was so nice and seemed so out of place compared to the other women that I usually chauffeured around. See, the predators liked the innocent women… To them, the challenge was like sleeping with a virgin on prom night. Prostitutes and women that were easy to sleep with were not enough to massage their egos. However, a newcomer in their inner circle was considered a much better score. The perverts would always choose a young and fresh woman in town over a used call girl. The predators viewed their libidos as cravings that were impossible to satisfy, no matter how hard they tried. The mansions and large estates made it so easy to lure these virginal women to the property. After all, many women were looking to experience the Hollywood and Beverly Hills lifestyle, especially if they were trying to get an acting career going. Oftentimes, these women associated someone owning a huge mansion to someone with contacts in the film industry… If only I could have told them that some of the homes were being rented.

I had an assignment one day to go to the Sunset Plaza home. The Doctor had told me that it looked like someone was living in one of his properties and had hammered a nail into two of his back doors. I told the Doctor to call the police, but he said that an ex-girlfriend had just moved out and he didn't want to escalate the situation in case it was because of her or one of her friends. So I armed up with my .45 Colt and went to check the house out. There was a nail in the garage door and when I knocked on the front door, no one answered. I unlocked the door with my key, and a middle-aged man from inside began to charge at me and pull out a black .38 revolver as he screamed, "Who the hell are you?" I showed the man my badge and ID as I pulled out my own pistol and told him that the owners sent me. The man's girlfriend came flying downstairs while brandishing her .25 auto pistol and we all just stood there, looking at each other with our guns drawn. The man explained to me that he had rented the home for a month from the owner, and I asked him if I could see the lease. He produced a lease, and there it was in black and white, with the Producer's name on it.

We all put our guns away and I made a call to the Doctor. He instructed me to drive to the Producer's home and tell him what had happened. When I arrived at the Producer's, he was waiting with an envelope full of one-hundred-dollar bills for the Doctor. The Doctor had called the Producer on my way over and the Producer apologized for not telling him he had leased the house to a friend. The Producer gave me some money and two tickets to a concert at the Hollywood Bowl for my troubles. As much as I enjoyed the money and the Hollywood Bowl tickets, I couldn't stop thinking that I could have died over a simple miscommunication. I am sure people have gotten shot or died from similar situations… just a big disconnection while everyone is frantically doing favors and making money.

On a separate day, a new client had assigned me to go with him to Beverly Hills to sell some jewelry to a female business partner. We went up to a large estate and the front gate opened for us. Two bodyguards came outside and asked if I was armed. I told them that of course I was and showed them my ID. They told me to leave my gun in the car and I looked at my client as if two idiots were speaking to me. I told the bodyguards that I will not do that and that I am paid to do the same job that they were, so they should probably let us in so we could get the job done. After passing the dumbshit test, we all entered the estate. My client's attractive business partner greeted us and asked if anyone would like a beer. We all declined. After the meeting, I was driving back with my client and he told me that he had just made his third $100,000 deal with the woman. He explained to me that the woman was always stoned and that she was married to a plastic surgeon. He paid me a bonus after that deal and was a client for three other occasions. It wasn't until later when I heard he had gotten caught sleeping with this female business partner at her estate, and she ended up getting into a heated divorce with the plastic surgeon. Afterward, I made a note to myself that the mansions were the best places to witness the fucked-up Hollywood scene.

# CHAPTER 15

# IT'S NOT WHO YOU KNOW

> *"Papa Don't Preach" by Madonna*

Hollywood is not about who you know, but how you know them. What many people don't realize is that business relationships make up the entertainment industry. When someone needs something from another party, the important part is what is needed. Does someone need something materialistic or do they need to meet a particular person? From these business relationships, various smaller relationships can be formed from them. After all, everyone wants to know or meet a famous star to build their status. When this is the environment you are living in, it is especially necessary for upcoming talent to establish contacts and connections within the industry. Sadly, this outgoing desire to meet people resulted in many people becoming exploited in Hollywood.

One night, I picked up the Doctor and he had two other beautiful women with him. Pixie, my friend and martial arts student, was one of them. I drove them all to Traps, a major upscale club in Beverly Hills. After parking the limo, we got right in because the Doctor was on the VIP list. We all entered the packed club and grabbed seats next to John Lennon's son, Julian. Julian was an absolutely enjoyable person, and it was really cool to see the interaction between him and the Doctor.

After about an hour, the Doctor told me that I was officially off duty, and he wanted me to dance with Pixie. Of course he was trying to set me up with her, and the inner group knew I had a thing for her. So we went to the dance floor and before I knew it, we were dancing next to a lovely goddess wearing a headband. Holy shit, it was Cher! We moved away from her and I bumped into a big black guy, who was a bodyguard for Prince. Prince was dancing with a tall black-haired lady, which was not hard to notice since he was relatively short and his classic high-heeled shoes did not make him look much taller. He looked just like he did on stage and in the movies; a real personality that drew you to stare. As we were staring at Prince, his bodyguard went to drag me away. Trying to open up some space for other dancers attempting to catch a peek, the bodyguard touched me near my waist and hit my .45 Colt. The bodyguard's eyes got wide and he turned toward me with a big smile. I said to him, "Yes, I am one of you." We got to dance between Cher and Prince for as long as we wanted. Talk about professional courtesy!

Name-dropping was the best way for people to get laid in Hollywood. Therefore, many people lied when they name-dropped… just to try and impress someone else. While driving or standing around bodyguarding, you get to be in the room when the lies start. I was in the office with the Doctor and the phone rang. It was one of the Sunset Plaza women. She was needy and wanted some money because she didn't have any means of support once her money from back home ran out. Not having a job, she was hoping that the Doctor could "lend" her some money. The Doctor told her that he had to take a call from a famous actor and would call her back. Now this was not necessarily a full lie because the Doctor did know some famous people, but the actor he alluded to being friends with was not in his inner circle. The Doctor picked up the phone and called the Producer, asking him if he could meet this supposed actor. Of course, a favor would be owed and he would be very grateful. He hung up the phone and called back the Sunset Plaza woman. "Come on over, and we will talk about it." Sunset Plaza Drive was about twenty-five minutes from the office, so the woman was standing ready and was over in half an hour. She entered the office with a smile and looking gorgeous, long blonde hair and red lipstick. She wore a low-cut blouse, a mini skirt, and shoe pumps. The Doctor asked me to leave and to shut the door behind me. Several minutes later, the door opened and the woman hugged me goodbye before leaving the building. I walked into the office and the Doctor was ecstatic. He bragged to me, "She has the tastiest pussy and was so tight!" He was like a high school teenager telling his friends about his sexual adventures.

I thought it was all so weird because the Sunset Plaza woman was obviously being taken advantage of, despite her not even realizing it. Simply because he had given her some money to last a few days and promised her that he would introduce her to some famous actor, I knew she now owed the Doctor favors. She was in no way a prostitute and she was always one of the most well-behaved women at the Sunset Plaza home. She was just in a bad position and had to make one of those fucked-up life choices. The next day, one of the Producer's assistants came by the office to pick up several Quaaludes from one of the storage lockers… fulfillment of the Doctor's end of the favor. Long story short, the Doctor met this famous actor but the Sunset Plaza woman was never given the opportunity. She had fallen victim to Hollywood's phony name-dropping motto: It's not who you know, but who you blow.

# CHAPTER 16

# HOLLYWOOD PORN

*"Maneater" by Daryl Hall and John Oates*

I felt it necessary to mention a few things to help further illustrate the stage of all this bizarre sexual energy in the eighties. Hustler magazine had moved its headquarters to Los Angeles and the world-famous Playboy Mansion was located in Hollywood. The porn industry was huge in Hollywood and so were the dicks. One of the most famous porn stars at the time was John Holmes, who died of AIDS in 1988. The title of his most famous adult film was Taxi Girls, considered a true classic. Overall, you could not go anywhere in Hollywood and not be reminded of sex. Sunset Boulevard had sex shops all along it and Hollywood Boulevard still openly displayed the old magazine racks of nude women. Escorts and dancers were also highly advertised throughout the city. If you wanted kinky, then you came to the right town.

Pornography was obviously not only exclusive to Los Angeles or Hollywood. However, if someone were looking to make really good money in the porn industry, they would want to work in Hollywood because it consisted of wealthy producers and other industry connections that no other city had. The orgies and wild sex parties my clients (and other wealthy elites) embellished with Quaaludes and cocaine definitely had an influence on porn as well. They even joked about their impact on the industry and gave themselves porn names to make it seem like their influence was acceptable. The open welcoming of porn was so crazy that even theatrical plays and comic strips of the day had material poking fun at it. The billions of dollars being made from porn began to intensify the challenge for newcomers to adapt in Hollywood. Even if you were a terrific actor and had never heard of Marilyn Monroe's life story, you would be thrown into a perverted life of sexually charged Hollywood culture. It was not just the eccentric and over-the-top lifestyle that gave Hollywood the nickname *Hollyweird.*

At night, the fashion of leather and lace was everywhere. On Vine Street you could find black transvestite escorts, while the sultry escorts cruised Hollywood Boulevard. There was even an S&M nightclub that was called Chateau, located on La Cienega Boulevard. I was amazed by how many times I had to pick up or drive clients to this location. Women referred to as "madams" worked the club, caging and bondaging those that wished to participate. I had a tour of the club once when one of my clients befriended a madam there. It was such a dark and twisted place that I felt my age jumped from twenty-six to thirty years old real quick. I kept expecting to see Elvira: Mistress of the Dark to jump out at me, but she seemed like a pussycat compared to the sadistic vixen there. I was glad I was armed with my pistol, and I couldn't be in more of a hurry to get out of there.

In 1986, the Attorney General's Commission on Pornography released the final draft of its report. Also known as the Meese Report, the report came to the conclusion that hardcore porn served as a connection to sexual harassment and organized crime. Although living in Hollywood at the time made me feel like there may be some truth to the report, the public deemed it as uncredible and biased propaganda. To this day, the report is never mentioned during cases of sexual abuse and has hardly even elevated to the importance of further study. People love their sex until someone gets hurt from it. We are sure to have a surplus of condoms and birth control for safe sex, but we seem to lack consulting and help for sex addicts. The entire hypersexual scene in Hollywood had become surreal, corrupted, and out of control.

# CHAPTER 17

# WHAT THE FUCK

> *"Just Like Paradise" by David Lee Roth*

One night, I was paged to head to the office as soon as possible. I had been in a weapons training facility in Orange County renewing my open carry permits, and I ran out of class as soon as I got the page. The Doctor needed me to pick him up from the office at 6:00 p.m. and get him to a club in Beverly Hills by 6:30 p.m. I was forty-five minutes away and had to dress into a suit while I drove… something I became really good at during my time in Hollywood. It wasn't very safe, but it was a great way to save time so that I could show up dressed and ready to go.

It was a crazy Friday night and the traffic was so shitty. I hit Western Avenue at 5:50 p.m. and was thirteen minutes from the office. I flew down the right side of the street, cutting off cars so that I could make it to the Doctor's office on time. I had been in Los Angeles for two years now and had begun to know my way around Western Avenue and other busy streets like Normandy and La Brea, but they were still always a mess to drive on when running late. I opened the limo passenger door at 6:15 p.m., and the Doctor entered. I began driving him to a restaurant and club known as The Fish Market. "What the fuck is up, Doc?" The Doctor told me that one of the most gorgeous Swedish gals he had been fascinated with for months was going to be at the club with her friends, and this was the night he was going to land her. After I parked the limo, he asked me to come in to hang out with him and the women. I knew then that I would be a decoy and that I would end up driving the Swedish gal's friends to anywhere they wanted once I had dropped her and the Doctor off. The Swedish gal was a really tall blonde, and her three friends were smaller but dressed really sexy. They were out for a night on the town and meant business.

After being at the club, everyone decided to go to the Rainbow Room. We all jumped into the limo and headed to our new club. When we pulled up to the club, the Swedish gal's friends jumped out and the Doctor told them to go ahead. When the Swedish gal's friends entered the club, the Doctor asked me to drive him and the Swedish gal to the office. After arriving at the Doctor's office, the Doctor told me that he could use his car from there and that I could leave them. They got out of the limo and went up to the Doctor's office to fuck. I drove back to the Rainbow Room and joined the women, who were sitting at a booth with two of the band members from Whitesnake. There we were. Two major rockers, three hot chicks, and a bodyguard with short hair and a blue suit. Conservatives, liberals, and artists all in one place… That was Hollywood for you.

I could tell that everyone at the table was high and that the levity in their conversations was just as high. Everyone was having a great time, and then the band members left. The women went upstairs to dance, and I went with them because I was used to late nights and was not tired. We met two guys and we all danced until 2:00 a.m. The women took a cab home and the guys we met invited me back to their house to talk about life and our different reasons for coming to Hollywood. Not having a lot of friends my own age, I accepted their offer. I drove the guys to their one-bedroom but well-furnished apartment. I sat on their couch and began drinking a Frangelico that they poured me. After about ten minutes, one of the guys sat down really close next to me. Right in the middle of one of my stories, the guy leaned over and tried to kiss me on the mouth. I stood straight up, not mad, just really startled. I walked out of the front door as I said to the guys, "I think there has been a misunderstanding." I had heard of bisexual activity, but this was the first time I witnessed it in Hollywood. When these dudes couldn't pull the women, they switched to the next new body… me. I could only think of one thing as I walked out to the limo: *What the fuck! I should have just stayed in Orange County!*

# CHAPTER 18

# GAME OF MANIPULATION

*"Head Games" by Foreigner*

Many people in their twenties and thirties were blowing off a lot of steam in the 1980s, and it became common for them to mix recreational drugs with narcotics as a way to intensify their experiences. Some of these participants had well-paid jobs, while others were not interested in living large. However, everyone was interested in experiencing the excessive Hollywood lifestyle of partying and impressing others. This vain and reputational way of life made Hollywood a town circulating around games of manipulation.

Hollywood had an endless supply of young impressionists that did not have the years of experience to separate the bullshit from reality. Along with a Quaalude or some magic powder with endless amounts of alcohol, a savvy older person could manipulate his way into your pants before you even knew it. Similar to when a professional pickpocket has his target in sight and deems them the "mark," my clients viewed a young virgin that had just come to town in the same way. Oftentimes the mark wasn't literally a virgin, but they would be in my clients' crosshairs because of their clean and innocent background. I was paged often to pick up these naive impressionists, which my older clients claimed they wanted to help. In the end, most of my clients just wanted to impress their mark so that they could get their victim's guard down.

I remember one night I was driving a young, naive woman to a party. I was now two years into the Hollywood scene and I knew the Producer really wanted to fuck this chick. I was still pissed off at the Producer from being set up into going to the Sunset Plaza home and almost getting into a gunfight, so I took a big risk. I warned the woman to watch out for the Producer's moves and to only drink what she poured for herself. I insisted to the woman, "Drink as much as you want now if it is a buzz you want, but do not drink at the party. You can have some leftover coke from the last client I drove, or even take what you want from the limo bar to put into your purse." The woman began to get weirded out and asked me why I was telling her all this. I told her that I had a girlfriend and if I knew she was going into a place that may have spiked drinks, I would want someone to let her know. I gave her my pager number and told her to just enter "911," and I would be outside in half an hour to pick her up. I wanted to make it clear as possible to the woman that if the Producer fucked her, it would be because she consented to it.

About two hours later, I was leaving the office to go out to dinner with the Doctor when I got the page that said, "911." I came clean to the Doctor about the situation and since he and the Producer were friends, I thought I was going to get hell for it. However, without a second thought, the Doctor suggested that we take the woman out to dinner with us. I started laughing so hard that I almost missed my turn on Vine Street. The Doctor knew he had to meet this woman if the Producer wanted her so bad, and I felt like the vampire's helper setting up his next meal. But when we picked the woman up from the Producer's house, we went to dinner and danced for a few hours before dropping her off at her apartment. The Doctor just needed the amusement, and in a strange way he was playing his own game of manipulation with the Producer. By taking this woman away from the Producer, the Doctor felt it gained leverage over him. The more manipulation and leverage he had, the more powerful he felt.

I got into deep water with the Doctor one time when a competing helper threw me under the bus. He was a cameraman that was not doing so well, but the Doctor liked him and needed some videotaping done. One night, I grabbed the keys to the Doctor's Mustang and went to Orange County for a couple days to visit my girlfriend. It was not a totally bad thing because as a bodyguard I could drive any of the Doctor's cars available, but I was only supposed to stay in the Hollywood and Los Angeles areas when driving them. With the cameraman knowing this, he took down the mileage on the Mustang and indicated to the Doctor that the car had left Los Angeles. The cameraman really made big points with the Doctor after busting me, and he knew that it made his influence with the Doctor surpass mine. I knew I had to get the cameraman back, but later that month I didn't have to seek revenge against him because he ended up crashing the Doctor's Mercedes. I ended up back on the Doctor's A-list.

Games of manipulation even circulated around finances. During the big leagues of finance in the 1980s, the banks did not always cross-reference a secured line of credit. A client could use the same property to secure three bank loans with three different banks… Now you know why so many banks folded during the early 1990s recession. It was ruthless, but the bank's clients got large lines of credit to support their lifestyles and bad investments. I thought it was funny when the Doctor took out a $300,000 line of credit and started writing a check that evening to buy his girlfriend a car. I jokingly told the Doctor, "Don't you think that is dangerous? I don't think you're going to be with her for too long." He responded to me with one of his most memorable lines, "Roger, have you heard of spending money like there's no tomorrow?" I told him that I had. He ended the conversation by saying, "Well, I have very little tomorrow left. So I'm spending it!"

# CHAPTER 19

# SELF-INDULGENCE MAKES THE WORLD GO ROUND

*"Money" by The Flying Lizards*

I moved to Hollywood mainly for lucrative purposes. Aside from that, I was also stimulated by the fast-paced environment and the unique lifestyle any man in his twenties would want to experience. I had a strange sense of duty and a need to help people, but I did not want to join the military. I enjoyed taking care of people and being around wealthy, influential big shots (which was not a bad thing for a young person just starting their career). I quickly learned that not everyone with money shared it or used it for philanthropic purposes. Growing up, I felt that money was a magic wand that provided people with happiness and fulfilled desires. When I moved to Hollywood, I realized that the wealthy didn't even need to spend money to get what they wanted.

To entertain young women or impress people, wealthy elites would use their power and influence to have others provide them with drugs or favors. In the eighties, a limo driver may be called to pick up a drug dealer so that they could provide drugs to the party. The purpose of these drugs were to loosen up the party and allow people to explore their various feelings. But as we know, drugs don't always lead to a good time.

Many women in Hollywood took advantage of these wealthy people, knowing that they themselves would never make it in the film industry or make a proper living. Therefore, they knew that the only way to continue their lifestyles was through partying and taking drugs in big homes with rich guys. This Hollywood culture led many women down a vicious cycle where they would exchange favors for a way of sustaining their affluent lifestyle, despite them not having money to afford it. Aside from sexual favors, women knew that luring other beautiful girls into the group was an alternative way to sustain their cravings. This way of life resulted in many women exploiting each other so that they could continue to feed their addictions… many times not even realizing or acknowledging that this was an actual issue. Most of the time, these women would rather fuel their repetitive habits instead of seeking actual help for them.

# CHAPTER 20

# RAT PACK OR JUST RATS?

> *"Luck Be a Lady" by Frank Sinatra*

The Rat Pack was a musical entertainment group featuring Frank Sinatra, Dean Martin, Sammy Davis Jr., Peter Lawford, and Joey Bishop. Even though the Rat Pack had been popular during the fifties and sixties, their songs and style lived on for generations and resonated with older people that admired them. The Rat Pack was known and loved mainly for their music. However, because of their womanizing scandals during their earlier years, they set the stage for becoming sex symbols. Many of my wealthy clients grew up during the Rat Pack days and, resembling their idols, they too developed their own platform to sleep with beautiful women. Whether it was through wealth or giving women the opportunity to be in movies or around famous people, my clients attempted to manipulate women in any way possible. Their unprincipled formula revolved heavily around the party scene in Hollywood.

Drugs were so affiliated with the culture that it seemed normal to partake in them without realizing their detrimental effects. Sex and drugs had become essential tools for releasing dopamine and boosting our sense of pleasure. It was well known that having Quaaludes or a supply of cocaine could increase your chances of sleeping with your date. If your date was high or in a state of grandeur, then it increased the ability for you to take advantage of them. Mickeys and other sleeping pills were slipped into cocktail drinks to bring down their victim's guard and make them vulnerable. Other drugs, such as the Spanish Fly, were used as aphrodisiacs to directly arouse both men and women. The seemingly normal Hollywood culture not only evolved toward becoming a rape culture, but it also increased sex and drug addiction with hardly any backlash or noticeability.

What was amazing was the fun that most people were having while others were being taken advantage of. While many people were having the time of their lives at self-indulging parties, they were clueless of the minority there that would end up being exploited. It is such a traumatic experience when you think you are with someone that wants to be your friend, but they end up taking advantage of you. I am sure we will only see a small portion of these victims bringing their stories to light, but there were numerous people that were abused under these similar circumstances.

There were a lot of bummers in Hollywood. Like any big city, there were a lot of nasty people that believed they were empowered and no one was going to convince them otherwise. One day, I was driving a client to the airport and he was telling me more than I needed to know. He was bragging to me about a beautiful woman that he seduced by getting her drunk and doped up at a party. In his mind, he really believed she was a lucky gal to have been shown such a good time. On my way back to the office, I took a side street while contemplating what that asshole had told me. Delusional—he considered himself as someone that was respectable no matter how manipulative and scandalous he behaved… He thought of himself as a member of the Rat Pack, being loved by everyone yet requiring a distorted platform to sleep with women. That week, I visited my parents' home in Orange County so that I could take a break and get a chance to clear my head from all the Hollywood craziness.

# CHAPTER 21

# WHAT HAPPENS IN HOLLYWOOD DOESN'T STAY IN HOLLYWOOD

> *"Take On Me" by A-ha*

If you think Las Vegas is *Sin City*, then Los Angeles should have been deemed *Nefarious City*. Similar to any big city, all the new and exciting things that people enjoy will travel with them. I was given a plane ticket to Cannes, France by the Doctor and he told me to be at his home in six days to help him pack. We were going to the Cannes Film Festival and were going to stay in a villa that he had rented on the southern coast of France. We were excited to visit Monaco, a small sovereign state north of Cannes. Specifically, Monte Carlo was a common district for Hollywood stars to travel to and gamble.

We boarded the TWA flight and off we went. I had been to Europe before, but never with the Doctor or any of my clients on a first class flight. I was excited to finally get a chance to use my training internationally. The Doctor wanted me to work five days driving him and have two days off for myself. He was paying me for overtime, and he had rented a small Mercedes-Benz C-Class for me to drive him and his guests around. Once our flight landed, we drove straight to our villa. As soon as we arrived, we noticed that three women from our entourage were already there. The women were already higher than ever and they greeted us with hugs. The villa reminded me of the Sunset Plaza home, three stories tall with a pool outside.

The scene was just like Hollywood, a party a night and going out to clubs with A-list people. Whisky a Go Go even had a club there and was our favorite place during the whole week. It seemed liked everywhere we went, there was partying, dancing, and pills. See, when traveling during the 1980s, the best thing to take was pills. European countries had strict laws when it came to importing drugs, but pills were much less likely to be questioned in those days. So there we were in Monte Carlo with as many Quaaludes, Valium, amphetamines, and painkillers that we could ever wish for.

Monaco was beautiful and so were the people there. It was like Hollywood in France with a harbor full of yachts and large boats. I met Dar Robinson one morning, the famous stuntman that broke and set world records. When passing by our villa, he noticed I was doing karate on the grassy area in front of our pool. He liked that I was a black belt and we talked about the stunt business. The Gulf War was right around the corner, so the USS America happened to be in the harbor. Being a part of a celebrity crew, we were able to set up a tour of the aircraft carrier. When we boarded the ship for our tour, the crew knew Dar's name from the movies and they gave him a really nice welcome. After the tour, we went back to town to have dinner and party some more. Before the trip, the Doctor had invested in an independent film to be produced and spent about $300,000 for the Rights of the Producer. The film never made it past production; however, that didn't stop the Doctor from discussing it to seem legitimate when meeting women and other Hollywood types in Monaco.

On my first day off, I was walking around town and having a really great time until my pager went off displaying "911." *Wow! Here? Really?!* I immediately returned to the villa. The Doctor and the Producer were there and, without going into specifics, they told me I had to go to the border of Italy and France to pick up one of the young gals of our entourage from the police station. I suited up, got my passport and security ID, and drove to the police station. I didn't speak French, so the French police had an English-speaking policewoman take me to an interrogation room… The gal from our entourage was nowhere in sight. Two gendarmes came in and stood with the policewoman, one of them holding a machine gun. I was really impressed with these guys. Everything I heard about the gendarme turned out to be true; all of them are totally professional and you do not want to fuck with them.

The French police asked me several questions regarding who I was and what relationship I had with the gal from our entourage. I told them that I was a licensed bodyguard and driver for a Hollywood film crew that hired me to pick her up. I went on to tell them that I had a letter from the film company, stating that any information can be directed to their attorney back in America. The French police were not happy, but nonetheless they sent another gendarme into my interrogation room. This gendarme sat down and thanked me for coming to get the gal. I told him that it was my job and that I was instructed to help in any way. He went on tell me that the gal from our entourage had been partying and was picked up by two men who were acting like her friends. They drove her across the border to Italy, where they went on to beat and rape her.

My mouth dropped open, and I could not believe the Doctor and the Producer had set me up… They wanted no part of this shit. I told the gendarme that I would be happy to take the gal back home to America and he said that would be fine. The gendarme finally brought the gal out, and I was instructed to call our villa from the nearest phone and speak to the Doctor. He and the Producer had already scheduled a doctor's appointment for the gal and bought her a plane ticket home. After taking the gal to a doctor and back to the villa to get her belongings, I drove her to the airport. She hugged and thanked me before getting on her flight back to America. For many days, I couldn't stop thinking about the incident and how bad I felt for the gal. I never ended up seeing her again when I returned to Los Angeles.

Palm Springs—the fuck capital for Hollywood stars that wanted to get out of town for some fast recreation. It was a shorter drive than Vegas and its relaxing weather made it a glamorous destination for many celebrities. If you were married and had a big home in Hollywood or Beverly Hills, this was a great place to golf, swim, get a massage, or hang out with your friends for a weekend. However, Palm Springs was also a common destination to take women to party and have sex all weekend. The parties in Palm Springs were not so abundant in the sixties and seventies; but by the eighties, it had become the ideal place to let loose.

I drove my clients to Palm Springs often and about one out of every three trips there was with their steady girlfriend or wife. I always enjoyed these scarce trips because they led to much less drama. On the other two out of three trips, a client would bring a number of young women with them. Almost always, these trips turned into drama that would make the craziest reality shows look like church sessions. Many times we took two vehicles on our trips (with the women in the limo and the client in one of the private cars), just in case the client ended up leaving early because of the drama. The young women would always drink and overindulge on drugs, making the drive louder and not as relaxing. If someone was having a bad trip or if the client did not get laid or sucked off, there was bound to be trouble and I would have to hear about it from both sides. All the way back from the trip, the women would ask me if I knew that the client wanted to sleep with them. I would often respond, saying, "I am sorry. I just work for him." Sometimes if I was feeling ballsy or on edge, I would respond asking them if they thought they were invited because of their deep academic discussions.

You have to understand that I was with these women for months at a time, being rotated in and out of the lives of a client. Looking back, there would be times when I would get fed up with clients or from the bellyaching of the young women. It was not a glamorous job, and there were times when it got overwhelming or even frustrating. However, the job paid well and I did not complain much about it in my mid-twenties. In fact, many times I felt fortunate to have the job because I got the opportunity to go to cool places and hang out with celebrities or wealthy people. I guess I just kept an optimistic mindset, outweighing the atrocities with the benefits.

# CHAPTER 22

# LOVE ME TWO TIMES

*"It's My Life" by Talk Talk*

During 1987, I was motivated to make some extra spending money. I started working overtime, working up to twenty hours on some days. One morning, I went to go check on the Sunset Plaza house and pick up Pixie. As I pulled up to the house, I saw a guy around my same age leaving from the front door. I got out of the limo and kindly said hello to him, but he jumped into my shit. He screamed at me, "Who the fuck are you?"

I got into a defensive posture and pulled my badge out. "I work for the owners… And now I have to ask you what you're doing on this property." He aggressively charged at me and tried to push me, but I took his weight in and flipped him onto his back with my knee in his chest. Suddenly, the front door opened again and Pixie stepped outside. She told me that the guy was her guest and she begged me not to hurt him, so I let him up. As soon as he got on his feet, he took a swing at me, and down he went again. I got in the man's face. "What hell are you doing? You're trespassing and you just committed assault and battery. If you do not stop this shit, I will call the police." Pixie pleaded for me to let him go and to not call the police. I told the guy in a soft voice, "I am going to let you back up. But if you do not go, I will have you arrested." He responded that he was the one that was going to have me arrested. So I took my handcuffs out of my pocket and flipped his ass over. He started to struggle, but I was twice his strength and had his arm extended out and locked. He screamed for help and the other two women staying in the Sunset Plaza home came running outside. The women yelled at the man to shut up and implored me to not hurt him. Just before I cuffed the dickhead, he calmed down and said that he just had a really bad hangover… as if that was the reason he was being hostile. I eventually uncuffed the guy and let him up. As I began putting my handcuffs away, my suit jacket flapped open and he saw my holstered gun. Realizing I could have shot him if I wanted to, he immediately began throwing up in the front yard. The women got him a glass of water before he got on his motorcycle and drove off.

Pixie and the women begged me not to tell the Doctor or the Producer about their guest. I liked Pixie and told the women that I would not say anything this time, but I warned them that I would have to if any other overnight guests ended up staying over. I knew it was my ass on the line if I didn't report these infractions to the Doctor. Pixie told me that she was dating the guy and that normally he was much nicer, but she told him that she had to go to Palm Springs with the Doctor. The guy ended up getting jealous and he did not like the idea of her fucking two different guys. I smiled and agreed that that would make me angry as well. Pixie was just trying to please her sponsors, but at the same time she liked this younger guy who was trying to make it in the movies. I told her that I didn't really want to break the guy's arm anyway and if she could be ready in fifteen minutes, I could give her a ride to the office to see the Doctor. She told me that I was a doll and asked me in for a cup of coffee. I went in and went up to the little kitchenette that was set up downstairs. The other two women were acting weird and the house looked like they had been partying all night. Then a bedroom door opened and another guy walked into the kitchen… The women just looked at me and smiled. I said, "Is it me or is that another guy that stayed over last night?" The women were just being twenty-year-olds, sneaking guys in and out behind their sponsors' backs like teenagers keeping secrets from their father. This second guy looked at me and I was thinking that he had to have heard the crazy commotion between me and the first guy, hoping to get out of the house as soon as possible. He was just another aspiring actor. Later that year, I ended up seeing him as an extra on General Hospital.

Pixie and I got into the limo and off we went to the office. We got there and waited for the Doctor for about an hour. When the Doctor arrived, he gave me instructions to go pick up one of his friends at the airport before he went into an exam room with Pixie. On my drive to the airport, I was thinking that the woman had just left her young lover this morning and now she was already going at it again with her sponsor. "Love Me Two Times" by the Doors came on the radio and I broke out laughing so hard that I nearly sideswiped a bus. I arrived at the airport and picked up an elder gentleman that did real estate business with the Doctor. He was known to be a land development and acquisition expert. I did not know it then, but he would later become my mentor and an important part of me getting out of Los Angeles some years later. We went to the Holiday Inn and checked him in before grabbing breakfast. The Doctor and Pixie came into the lobby and met the gentleman in there. The reunion was joyful and the Doctor loved showing off this hot, young woman on his arm. Like many of the people the Doctor did business with, the gentleman was married and had a wife and kids… faithful for many years. The Doctor's business partners often had to come in town to do business and become exposed to the Hollywood lifestyle. However, the Doctor's business partners were always polar opposites of the Doctor himself, and this was the brilliance of him! The Doctor got experts for all the professions he needed, and this allowed him to live this amazing character of being himself. Everyone loved the Doctor's high-energy and amazingly eccentric personality.

I was asked to drop Pixie back off at the Sunset Plaza house and the guys went on to conduct their business. As we drove up to the Sunset Plaza home, there was her young boyfriend that I had cuffed just a few hours ago. He was sitting on the curb, waiting for her, and he stood up as I pulled the limo up to the house. Pixie asked me to please stay in the car and told me that she would explain to him that he needed to stop coming by. I saw them talk, when out of the side stairs came another dude from the lower apartment. I knew then that I had no choice but to tell the Doctor what was going on and as there had been many times before, there would be a housecleaning and a new set of young actresses would move into the lower apartment. But first, I was instructed to drop all three of the women off at the Producer's house that night for another pool party and skinny-dip.

# CHAPTER 23

# ROSES ARE RED, AND I WILL NOT WED

> *"Under Pressure" by Queen and David Bowie*

I am sure of one thing: the Producer did not want to get married. When Hugh Hefner (the iconic owner of Playboy Magazine) announced he was going to get married for a second time, my clients were assured that they would keep the sexual misbehavior of Hollywood partying alive and well. Many times my clients would say they had fallen in love with some of their favorite women, but at the end of the day they were only in love until the next cute women came into their circle… They could never be loyal to any woman. Most of my clients had been divorced at least once, and that may be the reason why they did not retry having long, meaningful relationships. In any case, my clients had beautiful women around them all the time (whether it was from their money, fame, or good bullshitting). They were not respectful to women and they lived to have their pleasures attended to. They said anything to keep the women coming back, no matter how many lies were needed.

During off-hours or while working, it was so interesting to hang out with the women and hear their perspectives on why they thought they would be the lucky one to marry one of my perverted clients. With all the drugs going into the women's systems, it was not a surprise that they would say the craziest shit. They were sold to the idea that they could be the one to settle down with one of my clients and convince them to change their ways… They were always disappointed.

On the top floor of the Sunset Plaza home, the Producer's master bedroom was for the one woman that we referred to as "going steady with their sponsor." A live-in girlfriend was not unusual while my clients were only seeing one woman, but they would always eventually go back to their proven ways of cycling between at least three women at a time. In return, my clients' girlfriends often had a false sense of stability and loyalty to them. The women would be spoiled for a while and even got some really nice gifts, but it was only a matter of time until they figured out that my clients were rotating them in and out of their lives for sex… just a short-term love affair to say the least. If you were a woman that could deal with two or three other women being around and you had the ability to be part of this entourage, you could probably stick around for a while. But if you had your own ego and competed to be the only woman in your sponsor's life, your shelf life was sixty days tops.

My clients never yelled or put the women down in my presence. They never got violent or argued with the women, no matter how mad the women may have gotten after learning their sponsor was just using them for sex or a way to get sex from their friends. One night, a short blonde escort got furious and started yelling and freaking out. My client kept his cool and just talked her down as we drove her to wherever she wanted to be dropped off. My clients did not put up with women that were hotheaded… It did not fall into the submissive sexual demeanor they liked from their pets.

When the women met other guys or got a steady boyfriend, my clients got even instead of getting jealous. If one of the women was found out to be having a boyfriend, even if they were sleeping with their sponsor, they did not last long. My clients had a very one-sided view of who was in control. I was always amazed how my clients would find out about the women's relationships. One day, the Doctor and I went to IHOP to get a chili omelet. Right there, in a booth by us, was one of the Sunset Plaza women with a young man. The Doctor said hello very politely and we sat down with them. The Doctor even picked up their check as if they were on friendly relations. I never saw the woman again at any party or client event.

# CHAPTER 24

# GENTLEMEN DON'T TELL

> *"She Drives Me Crazy" by Fine Young Cannibals*

When I was in high school, the boys would kiss and tell. My coaches would overhear and try to influence some sort of gentlemanlike behavior into us. They would say, "Gentlemen don't kiss and tell." I can tell you that in Hollywood, this was far from the truth. Hollywood was one giant place of gossip, usually when a new woman came into town and my clients had her in their crosshairs. They would obsess over trying to land her in their bed, limo, or casting couch… If they got a naked picture from her, that was considered a bonus. They would not only talk about how they exploited these women, but they would also take pride in it. Their conversations were always about some cute woman or hot deal they were working on. The fact that they had no class to truly realize that they resembled dirty, old perverts could make the most seasoned bodyguard blush.

A typical love story would often start off by qualifying how beautiful or over-the-top gorgeous the woman in the story was. However, one of my clients explained his love story a little differently at an eye-opening and memorable dinner I had with him.

My client: "We went to the Playboy Club for the show. Nadine was five foot eleven and all legs. I love a girl who is tall. Because when she spreads her legs, it is amazing to see those knees so high above her pussy. Her hair was so long and smelled so nice. I just kept smelling it all throughout the show. At dinner, I put my hand in her lap under the table and started fingering her clit while we necked. She was so hot and so wet. We had some piña colada and I gave her a Quaalude after our tiramisu. When we were heading into the limo to go dance on the strip, she pulled my dick out and started to stroke it before sucking it. I pulled her panties to the side and fingered her some more. I didn't cum, but I wanted to. After leaving the club, we went to the house and took a shower so she could play with herself in front of me. Then I bent her over the bed and rammed her over and over. She felt like a virgin and she tasted so good. I launched my cum on her asshole and we just clung onto each other all night."

I don't know how much of the story was embellished, if his date was wasted on drugs and booze, or if he actually had experienced a feisty night with a wild date looking to get ahead in Hollywood. My clients did not have any love for these women and it was all about outdoing the next guy… And if it wasn't about outdoing the next guy, it was about reliving their own perverted thoughts and trophy fucks.

Most of my clients had steady mistresses, either in Hollywood or out of town. They had the money to keep a steady gal in a condo or apartment, all while telling their side girlfriends that they were working late or having to travel for work. Having a bodyguard drive them, or just being around to appear working serenely, helped with their lies. The really crazy assignments I got were when I had to take the girlfriends out as a treat, so they got to use me as a bodyguard and limo driver. However, these "treats" were mainly meant for me to keep an eye on my client's girlfriend while he saw mistresses… It was like the old double standards we always heard about. I found it ironic when the girlfriends had me drive them directly to their side boyfriend's house. I remember one of the women looked me right in the eyes and said, "I know he is fucking around. So I am doing what I want to do and keeping my lifestyle as long as I can."

When the steady girlfriends told me their twisted sex stories as I was driving them around, I would always be reminded that this town was one wild ride. Should I say at this point that ladies don't kiss and tell either? Everyone was out for themselves and the times were about living every day as if it were your last.

# CHAPTER 25

# SHORT-TERM MEMORY

*"Your Love" by The Outfield*

I believe this is a good time to point out the numerous scandals that have come out regarding allegations in the eighties. I had been in a number of discussions with the Sunset Plaza women regarding their evenings with my clients. They were pissed because my clients claimed they would help further their careers, but ultimately ended up exploiting them. However, the women admitted that they had inferred they would have to go through these scenarios for them to scrape to the top… After all, getting a casting call that put them in a movie or television show was not easy. But when they were personally betrayed by these horny and manipulative old guys, this definitely soured their views on Hollywood. If they were lucky, they would get an agent or finish some credited acting classes so that they could potentially audition for more legitimate and upstanding casting calls.

During the stories I heard from the women, I realized that many times they wouldn't remember particular events or how the night would end. I started realizing this pattern when many of the stories would be slightly embellished or have parts omitted… And I don't think they did this because they were embarrassed to tell me about my clients being perverted. Based upon the environment during these times, I suspected that when a story got to the conversation about someone not remembering anything or saying, "Well, she went in the bedroom, and you know what happened," I was sure a Quaalude or roofie was involved.

I wanted to believe that my clients were just dating the women, trying to enjoy their company or help them meet people in Hollywood. However, when the women talked about not remembering large windows of the night, I began realizing more and more that they were being taken advantage of. Even scarier than this realization would be when the women themselves didn't realize it. I'd ask the women if they'd date my clients again, and most of the time they'd reply that they would. I began increasing my teaching of women's self-defense classes and emphasized to them even more about being aware of their environments.

Even my clients told me over-the-top stories, reminding me that they would not always have intercourse with the women. Their more wild stories consisted of telling me that they would only masturbate on the passed out women so that there would be no evidence of intercourse. It was as if these weird clients would premeditate their sick sex acts.

Many times when I'd got off work at three in the morning or later, I could not wind down. The women would be partying downstairs and when they'd ask me in for a drink, most of the time at least one of the them would be missing. I knew that their absence meant that they were either with a young boyfriend having consensual sex, or passed out in a mansion or hotel somewhere with one of my older clients. Because of this, I tried not to drink too much during the workweek because I wouldn't know if I'd be getting a page to go back out at night to pick up these missing women. I found it increasingly difficult to go out on the town or relax after a work night because I always dreaded still being on call.

# CHAPTER 26

# IF YOU CAN'T BEAT THEM, JOIN THEM

*"I Want A New Drug" by Huey Lewis*

When off work, I would spend my free time at clubs, hotels, restaurants, and A-list parties. I, myself, was no exception to the Hollywood party scene and indulged in occasional drinking as well. However, no matter where I went, drugs were always accessible. You did not even have to buy drugs if you were going to a well-stocked party, as the host would usually have or supply them. After spending three years in Los Angeles, and witnessing my affair with Hollywood, I felt that I deserved to unwind.

I worked out in those days and enjoyed being healthy. I trained often and was increasing my interest in martial arts. But when I would go out with friends or with my girlfriend, it was so easy to experiment. The possibilities to try different types of drugs did not stop with marijuana. This was Hollywood, man! It was not uncommon to have a pill to pick you up and another pill later to mellow you down. It seemed like everyone was willing to go down the rabbit hole without looking back.

I remember my first Quaalude. I was having a great visit with my girlfriend and she had been wondering about the effects of them. So, we had some drinks and both of us popped one each. About twenty minutes in, we were smiling and felt an amazing feeling of grandeur come over us. We felt the time roll by, like on Valium, but ten times more euphoric. We were so relaxed and joyful with everything around us. We felt like we were the only ones in the world that mattered. It was a wonderful night and I was really glad we experimented.

Cocaine was everywhere. I had done it with lovers and with rockers. Fortunately, I never enjoyed cocaine. After attending a family wedding in Chicago with my girlfriend, I decided that was the last time I would try it. We had done some coke and went to a nightclub. After getting really rowdy, the bouncers asked me to leave. I refused and they threw me out. This was not good enough for me, so I went back to complain to the manager. When five bouncers showed up at the door, I thought it would be a good idea to practice my karate. I held my own until one of the bouncers got me in a chokehold, and I was beginning to black out. I took an ink pin from out of my pocket and stabbed it under the bouncer's arm. He released me and I ran the fuck out of the club to my girlfriend's brother, who had the car running. We punched it and went back to the hotel. Twenty-four hours later, the local police came looking for me at the hotel. I had to use all my knowledge in bodyguard training just to keep my ass out of jail and get out of town. My girlfriend was so right when she said, "You got your ass kicked." After that, I flushed every speck of coke down the toilet. Coke did not help me make good decisions that night. From then on out, I would only allow myself to watch others snort the shit.

I was not done doing stupid stuff though. With the mid-eighties in full swing, I was now making some decent money. I traveled to exotic club resorts known for "hedonism week" destinations. They never advertised it, but I found out which ones to go to by asking the right people. I traveled to one of these resorts with my girlfriend and we met an exciting married couple. We partied for a week straight and I had my first orgy with them. It was an amazing resort with all consenting adults. The swimming, water sports, and club life had given me a false sense of reality. After having such a wild and joyful experience, I did not want to come home.

Now that New Age religion and media were pushing the envelope, many of the movies coming out were containing more sex, drugs, and radical living. It was these things that built the famous and iconic era of eighties culture. Films from the 1980s displayed a lot of chauvinistic ideology, containing what we would consider today as "politically incorrect" statements and behavior. More women were getting cast to play powerful roles, as if to ironically make up for how they were treated in real life. At the same time, the porn industry was evolving from less stag films to more comical or sexual plots with better graphics and higher budgets. During this transition, PG and R-rated films became more lenient toward violence and nudity.

Hollywood had become the new Wild West with drugs, sex, and wild parties ramping throughout the streets. People were exploring their deepest desires and adapting to the overindulging lifestyle. I remember so many overdoses being reported in the papers from people mixing alcohol with pills and cocaine. I guess I am blessed to have survived it.

# CHAPTER 27

# DON'T YOU DARE

> *"Whip It" by Devo*

The 1980s are considered a historic era not only for its life-changing events, but also for its dynamic lifestyles, cultures, and philosophies. Because of these rapidly evolving ways of life, there were many ironic things that made the era so unique and memorable. One of the most ironic things about the era was the development of the infamous DARE program by law enforcement.

Founded by Daryl Gates, chief of the Los Angeles Police Department from 1983 to 2009, DARE (Drug Abuse Resistance Education) was created to teach young adults about resisting drugs and violence. The prominent purpose of the program was to provide awareness on the dangers of drugs, therefore intending to discourage children from partaking in them. The program consisted of law enforcement going to schools and neighborhoods to educate young people about the poor choices of using drugs. The police officers that taught the program drove souped-up police cars with sirens and alloy wheels, the program's trademark DARE sign painted on the side of them. The program was honest and direct; however, it did have contradictive results.

Although the DARE program was revamped and still exists today, it did receive early backlash for turning young people onto drugs. Sociologist and psychiatrist, Richard Clayton, published a study in 1996 that concluded that the DARE program was ineffective. Summarized best by psychologist William Colson, Colson argued that the program's increased drug awareness motivated kids to become more curious of the drugs they were told not to take. The logic highlighted the paradox that people are more likely to try what they're told not to do. Designer drugs and crystal meth weren't even common in the eighties, but the program definitely helped spark their popularity. After all, if Adam and Eve couldn't resist the forbidden fruit, how are we expected to behave differently? The program was revamped to cover a more broader range of topics along the lines of influencing children to make healthier decisions.

The decadent and New Wave culture of 1980s Hollywood influenced eccentric and rebellious mentalities, driving people to yearn for an escape or alternate reality. These ironic hindrances, such as the DARE program, were no exception to the times. When we attempt to limit freedom and choice, little do we realize that we're unintentionally adding fuel to the fire.

# CHAPTER 28

# IF IT BLEEDS, IT READS

> *"Kiss Me Deadly" by Lita Ford*

When the police catch a killer, the killer is often arrested for one or two murders that they were accused of. However, it is usually only when the killer is thoroughly investigated until it is found out that they were associated with multiple murders and that they truly are a "serial" killer. Throughout the the eighties, there were a spree of serial killers that committed many horrific acts upon both men and woman within Los Angeles and other parts of the country. People were terrified of the fact that there were seemingly so many killers that would murder brutally, abundantly, and randomly. The entire country was kept in fear during the eighties under the media's constant coverage of the various killers on the loose.

Some of the most famous serial killers that stirred terror throughout the nation included Gary Ridgway, Jeffrey Dahmer, and Joseph James DeAngelo. A pattern or style of murder is associated to them as much as a favorite food or event is associated to each one of us. These sick bastards would commit home invasion, rape, torture, and murder simply for their own entertainment. Because of the unspeakable and dreadful acts serial killers were so capable of, the news spent countless amounts of effort keeping them in the spotlight.

A large reason that many of the sex scandals in Hollywood went unnoticed during the eighties is because they were belittled and whitewashed by the nonstop news coverage of serial killers and other "life-threatening" events. Similar to the AIDS epidemic coverage at the time, the media discovered that keeping their viewers fearful of death made for better television ratings and more captivating news. Coverage of death, violence, and conflict were prioritized over other events that didn't seem as urgent. Imagine it this way: Are the media and government agencies more likely to focus their time and resources on another woman being sexually assaulted, or a serial killer ruthlessly murdering their way through a state? The fact of the matter was that the severity of these sex scandals were being undermined and they weren't receiving the press coverage that they deserved. At the time, stories of sexual assault came off as white noise when everyone was so terrified of a psychopath on the loose. It's a shame how a greater evil can make the most immoral events look typical.

# CHAPTER 29

# SUPERPOWERS

> *"My Prerogative" by Bobby Brown*

It was a hot summer day in Hollywood when the Doctor paged me for the last time. He told me to be ready by 7:00 p.m. because it was his steady girlfriend's birthday. He had made reservations at a small restaurant in Burbank and invited a bunch of guests to join us. The rest of the guests and I showed up to the restaurant on time, but the Doctor and his girlfriend had not yet arrived. When the Doctor and his girlfriend finally walked into the restaurant, everyone exploded with excitement. The owner of the restaurant was all over our group, making sure we had everything we needed. Something I learned about the Doctor was that he provided a warm and comforting energy almost everywhere he went, as if he had superpowers. He was able to make people feel wonderful all the time, and he could have everyone eating out of his hand after just a minute of being around them.

I always considered the Doctor to have some sort of magic that I could not wrap my head around. I believed that the energy the Doctor harnessed was so intense, that people were constantly coming and going in his life because they could not keep up with his pace. The Doctor remembered your name by sight and could recall your favorite thing to do. He would compliment you on the way you looked, dressed, or spoke (even if it was unwarranted). He was truly a master of manipulation and had the ability to make people love him. I sometimes wondered if he had some sort of mind control or psychic powers to project what he wanted you to think or feel. Over the many days waiting for the Doctor at his Nichols Canyon home, I would notice his wide-ranging book collections. He would have medical, travel, and karate books mixed with textbooks that focused upon hypnosis, neurolinguistic programming, and witchcraft. Like a moth to a flame, I became fascinated with the Doctor and I began reading some of his books. Combined with these topics and my later study of Chi energy, I became convinced that everything we do effects an energy field in the universe. I've met with many academic scholars in science and quantum physics that believe mental power is unfathomable, but I was convinced that the Doctor had a gift in it.

The reason I am explaining all this is because I had great respect for the Doctor. He had single-handedly brought me into Hollywood and would continue to help my career even twenty years later. Over the relatively short period of time I spent bodyguarding and chauffeuring for the Doctor, he helped countless people financially, medically, and emotionally. Even after witnessing the worst of the Doctor and all the horrific events in Hollywood, I had developed an affection for him and a bond that is unexplainable.

No matter how it all turned out in the end, I have no regrets regarding my time in Hollywood. When I first got the job from the Doctor, I considered it as a sign of good karma being paid off. The ability to live in an area that was so exciting, wealthy, and interesting helped me distinguish what I did and didn't enjoy in life. The constant sexual energy in Hollywood was exhilarating, but the backstabbing and manipulation was too fatiguing. I do know for a fact that my time with the Doctor in Hollywood increased my knowledge of life, making me grow mentally and physically. My experience with the Doctor made me focus upon the good behavior that I wanted to emulate, and the substandard behavior that I wanted to avoid or improve upon. He had provided me the opportunity to experience the worst of people and the best of people during one of the most iconic times in Los Angeles.

# CHAPTER 30

# THE LAST DANCE

*"In the Air Tonight" by Phil Collins*

The Sunset Plaza home was eventually cleaned out and it became a long-term rental. The Doctor began living in it temporarily because the Nichols Canyon home reminded him too much of his steady girlfriend, the love of his life who he had finally broken up with. One night, he invited two women from Canada over. The Doctor entertained them with champagne and vodka while he had his standard one drink of Drambuie, a golden scotch whiskey mixed with honey and spices. I stayed to even out the party and overall it turned out to be a mellow evening. We did not go out on the town like most nights because the women had an early flight back to Canada the next morning, but we did have several drinks and the women had each taken a Quaalude earlier in the day.

The night progressed and the Doctor took one of the women into his bedroom. I was left alone with this attractive woman, but we had almost nothing in common except that we both didn't want to go to bed. We stayed up until 1:00 a.m. and ended up lying down in the blue room. We took off our clothes, did a quick feel up of each other, then turned away and went to sleep. The next morning, since I was supposed to drive the Doctor to the office, a limo came by and drove the women to the airport. I never saw those two women again, nor did I ever see my gold ring and one of my favorite leather coats that I had the previous night. I am positive that some boyfriend ended up getting them as nice gifts upon their girlfriend's return to Canada. My affair with Hollywood had started looking more like a divorce.

A growing concern from the Doctor had been hovering for months over whether I was to continue to assist him in Hollywood. I am sure the Doctor had sensed my disapproval of his treatment to the new women coming in and out of his circle of influence, along with my growing dislike for the Producer and some of the other clients in his inner circle. Now that Sunset Plaza was cleaned out of up-and-coming actresses, the Doctor decided to redefine my role to doing more administration for his real estate company and less bodyguarding. When I was sent to Sacramento to work on his real estate company's new acquisitions, I knew it was just a matter of time until the Doctor terminated my employment.

Despite my impending unemployment, I enjoyed the role the Doctor had me doing with his real estate company. I was working closely with the partners of the company and was learning the real estate profession, which I would later follow as a career. But at the time, I was young and naive. I was asked to get appraisals done and to return them directly to the Doctor in Los Angeles. One Monday morning, the senior partner of the company picked me up and he drove me to the Sacramento Airport to fly back to Los Angeles. On the way there, I was so excited that the appraisals came in high and that we were doing so well regarding the cash flow of the portfolio, that I boasted about it to the senior partner. Unfortunately, the partner had no clue that any appraisals were being completed and that the Doctor was refinancing the properties without his knowledge. By the time I landed in Los Angeles, the dear Doctor had a shitstorm of calls from the partners of the company. He chastised me for talking to the partners about the appraisals and he decided that that was to be the last month I was to work for him.

The Doctor gave me a small severance package to move back home to Orange County and he terminated all company business that I was originally involved with. I managed to obtain two rental properties that I planned to sell, hoping to build a small portfolio myself. I sold those houses and crawled back to Orange County. I never saw the Doctor again until his funeral a few years later. He died from exactly what he predicted he would—pancreatic cancer. As the Doctor lay in his casket, I remember recalling that it was the first time I didn't recognize his outgoing personality that I had known for so many years. It was depressing but stoic to see him lying down and looking so peaceful, two things that the Doctor strove never to do. I remember asking the last person that saw the Doctor alive if he was dancing when he died, but I never got an answer. I thought to myself that this was his last dance…

I do not know why I wept on the way home from the funeral. I was still so mad at the Doctor for terminating me and being an asshole at the end of our run. I think it was mainly from shock, knowing that it was the end of an era, and the death of this bright burning sun proved it. I knew inside that the Doctor had opened my eyes to a world I would have never seen, and he had helped push me to become a better human being.

# CHAPTER 31

# THE EYE-OPENING

*"If She Knew What She Wants" by The Bangles*

After witnessing these bad apples allure and manipulate various women during my short period of time in Hollywood, it is no wonder why so many scandals and allegations keep coming out regarding this era. At the time, the 1980s was known as a free-spirited period to make the most out of your life and to push the boundaries of entertainment. It is truly unfortunate that a handful of both men and women chose to abuse the culture and turn to devious acts to fulfill their lust, especially during such an exciting and eccentric time in history.

I began building an excellent self-defense program to teach men and women how to defend themselves. The opening section that I teach my students is about awareness and how to always understand your surroundings. The physical side of self-defense is the last thing you need to do if you do not use basic survival skills. I often point out to my students that there are some people that will do anything in their power to harm you or take advantage of you. My hope is to teach observation skills to help avoid people from getting into a scene where they feel trapped or useless. The most important thing I can teach my new students is the emotional and psychological forces within you and your opponent. It takes more to understand these factors than throwing a good kick at someone.

In closing, I would like to say that I hope ill-natured people will no longer prey upon the innocent... but we need to be realistic. There will always be manipulators, opportunists, and immoral people that we have to learn to spot. We need to educate and encourage younger people to not be afraid of living fun and exciting lives. We can teach them what to look out for, while at the same time teaching them that people make bad decisions when they demonstrate compulsive and irrational behavior. Many young people have so much energy and while thinking that they are pursuing entertainment, they can find themselves in terrible situations, especially if drugs, alcohol, and sex are involved.

The old saying by Oscar Wilde, "Everything in moderation" is the best course of action. During my time in Hollywood, I was overwhelmed and eagerly ambitious. Watching where I leaped helped me later in life when I learned to slow down. Opportunities come to you when you don't compromise your principles or follow manipulators. We should all strive to have healthy relationships while procuring and following our passions.

America is an amazing place to live and we should all enjoy our freedoms provided to us. With so much information available to us, we have the ability to understand and learn from the past in order to help each one of us prosper. I hope our culture can use education to make it more difficult for ill-minded people to take advantage of anyone else that is up-and-coming. I am far from the naive kid I was in Hollywood and I know now that there are people that will always be manipulative toward each other, but I hope we can help change the world by setting better examples. A few life lessons I learned in understanding human nature include knowing that the young will be impressionable, that creative minds will explore extremes, and that everyone has a large variety of opinions.

Roger in 1984.

# ABOUT THE AUTHOR

Roger Niez was born in Hawthorne, California in 1960. He was raised in Orange County with two older brothers by Polish-Catholic parents. After graduating high school as an all-American in football and wrestling, Roger started studying martial arts while attending college. In 1984, he saw an ad by a private-investigation company for bodyguards needed for the 1984 Olympics. He started their training program and began learning professional driving, countersurveillance, and executive protection. After several assignments, Roger moved to Los Angeles and opened a small office in a client's medical building. The journey he would go on over the next four years will not only amaze Roger, but also present him with experiences that wouldn't be acknowledged until nearly forty years later.

Roger is an author, businessman, and master martial artist who left Hollywood to develop a commercial real estate career. He survived three divorces, is happily married, and has two children. Roger is honored to share his early life stories as a bodyguard and limo driver in Los Angeles during the 1980s. He has great hopes that this book conveys a greater understanding of the historical era in Hollywood and teaches life lessons he learned from experience.